"You wanted eve̶[...] Brick," Lisa said. "No [...]

"I did," he confesse̶[...] "But tell me one time I [...]rested in you. As a friend, as a business woman, as a lover. Heck, as a woman who backs her car into something new on a weekly basis. Name one time."

Her eyes were wide with trepidation as he tucked his thumb under her chin and made her meet his gaze. He wanted them wide with wonder. He wanted to kiss her, to match her mouth to his, and to end this battling between them.

He did the next best thing to a kiss and rubbed his thumb across her lips. Back and forth, back and forth, until he gently pressed his finger into her mouth, then lifted it to his lips. "You can't name a time, because there's never been one," he whispered hoarsely. "In a minute we're getting out of this car, and I can't think about you anymore. Can't think about how much I want to hold you. About how I'd like to kiss you for the next hour and not come up for air. I can't think about how you feel under that T-shirt and those jeans and how much I've missed touching you, or I could screw up this job."

Her head was spinning, and her lips still burned from his touch as he pulled her from the car. She didn't think she'd ever recover from hearing Brick say those things. . . .

WHAT ARE *LOVESWEPT* ROMANCES?

They are stories of true romance and touching emotion. We believe those two very important ingredients are constants in our highly sensual and very believable stories in the LOVESWEPT line. Our goal is to give you, the reader, stories of consistently high quality that may sometimes make you laugh, sometimes make you cry, but are always fresh and creative and contain many delightful surprises within their pages.

Most romance fans read an enormous number of books. Those they truly love, they keep. Others may be traded with friends and soon forgotten. We hope that each LOVESWEPT romance will be a treasure—a "keeper." We will always try to publish

LOVE STORIES YOU'LL NEVER FORGET
BY AUTHORS YOU'LL ALWAYS REMEMBER

The Editors

PLAYING
WITH
DYNAMITE

LEANNE
BANKS

BANTAM BOOKS
NEW YORK · TORONTO · LONDON · SYDNEY · AUCKLAND

PLAYING WITH DYNAMITE
A Bantam Book / July 1994

If you would be interested in receiving protective vinyl covers for your Loveswept books, please write to this address for information:

Loveswept
Bantam Books
P.O. Box 985
Hicksville, NY 11802

ISBN 0-553-44384-4

Published simultaneously in the United States and Canada

Bantam Books are published by Bantam Books, a division of Bantam Doubleday Dell Publishing Group, Inc. Its trademark, consisting of the words "Bantam Books" and the portrayal of a rooster, is Registered in U.S. Patent and Trademark Office and in other countries. Marca Registrada. Bantam Books, 1540 Broadway, New York, New York 10036.

PRINTED IN THE UNITED STATES OF AMERICA

OPM   0 9 8 7 6 5 4 3 2 1

This book is dedicated
to all who feel the fear . . .
and do it anyway.

AUTHOR'S NOTE

The technical knowledge required for blasting with explosives covers the gamut of chemistry, engineering, geology, etc. . . . Amazingly enough, a certified blaster learns his craft primarily through on-the-job training instead of books. This could have made my research for *Playing with Dynamite* very difficult if I hadn't had access to Dennis Gould, technical consultant/certified blaster extraordinaire of Piedmont Explosives. Thank you, Dennis, for your patience and generosity. I must also thank the Demolition Contractors' Association of America for sharing information, and Alexander/Scott Inc. for providing pictures of nonelectric detonators. For clarification on another issue broached in this book, I'd like to thank the Anxiety Disorders Association of America.

ONE

"It's time to fish or cut bait, Brick."

Lisa Ransom's husky voice seeped through Brick Pendleton's mind at some semiconscious level. Several moments had passed, yet his body still pulsed with the exquisite sensations of sexual release. Their lovemaking had seemed even more intense than usual.

He had seduced her with persistence and care until she had turned the tables and *her* hands had gently inflamed him. The heady scent of her arousal had narrowed his awareness to her and only her. Her soft gasp of pleasure as he sank his hard flesh deep into hers had torn at his control, but it had been the signs of her climax both inside and out that had put him straight over the edge. When Lisa held him, she held him with her smooth thighs, her moist femininity, her trembling arms, and with the dazed satisfaction on her face. She held him with everything.

At the moment, he could identify with the buildings he demolished every day. He felt gloriously wasted, and he'd loved every minute of it.

He reached for the woman responsible for his current state of sensual repletion and his hand encountered her foot. He frowned, his sense of well-being abruptly altered. She had apparently sat up in bed.

Fish or cut bait.

"Fish?" he repeated, pulling his hand back and rubbing his face in an effort to clear his head.

"Yes," she said in a tense way that caused a sinking sensation in his gut. He had an uncomfortable premonition about what was coming. Reluctantly, he shook off his sexual lethargy and sat up in bed too.

"It's what I was trying to tell you before you— before we—" Lisa exhaled in frustration. "Before we ended up here. I've tried to tell you, but you always managed to distract me. Brick, I want a baby."

His breath lodged somewhere between his heart and throat. He stared at Lisa. Her long brown hair tumbled past her shoulders to the rose-colored sheet she clenched above her breasts. In the last six months, he'd made it his personal mission to learn every one of the five feet ten inches that comprised her luscious body, including the inches concealed by that cotton sheet. He knew she possessed the hourglass figure of his secret dreams along with a sweet, sensual generosity that had always brought him the greatest satisfaction.

Plus, she wasn't the least bit intimidated by his large size, and since Brick was over six three, he was accustomed to women being intimidated by him. Lisa, however, was fascinated by his size, and it had been his ultimate pleasure to indulge her fascination.

Touching her aroused his most primitive sexual instincts to a fever pitch. Exploring her personality... well, it sounded kind of smarmy, but the woman made him smile. He liked making her blush and laugh. And though he'd have a tough time explaining it, he liked the slightly awkward way she tried to make him welcome in her home. He worried that others would take advantage of her kind nature, so it was natural that he felt protective of her. With the exception of this baby thing she'd been hinting about for the last two months, Brick had been more than satisfied with their relationship.

He studied her face, noting that her lips were puffy from his kisses and she wasn't smiling. Her usually warm green eyes were clouded with a faint sadness. And she'd just told him she wanted a baby. A sick feeling settled low in his belly.

"Baby?" He'd hoped this was a passing phase. He reached over the side of the bed for the roll of antacids in his jeans' pocket. "You've got plenty of time to have a baby. You're just twenty-nine and—"

"Thirty."

Brick jerked back around to stare at her. "You didn't tell me. When was your birthday?"

She pulled the sheet up higher on her chest. "A week and a half ago. You were out of town for three weeks on that special job for the Andersons."

Discomfort simmered inside him. He'd been seeing Lisa for nine months, and for the last six they'd been intimate. He should have known when she'd had her birthday. Why hadn't he thought to ask? "I called you when I was gone. You didn't mention it."

Lisa gave a little shrug. "You didn't ask, and you didn't call that particular day."

Feeling as if he was a day late and a dollar short, Brick shook his head. "I sure as hell wish I had. Well, what did you do? Go to your parents' and celebrate?"

Lisa's eyelashes swept down like shutters over her eyes. "No. Senada gave me a little party."

Lisa's business partner, Senada, was one more reason for Brick to be chewing antacids. The woman was wild, and he didn't particularly like her influence over Lisa. Despite her age, Lisa had a rare innocence about her that appealed greatly to Brick. "What kind of little party?"

"It wasn't that big of a deal. She and a few other friends surprised me at the office."

"She probably brought in an army of male strippers," Brick muttered under his breath.

"Only one," Lisa countered. She must have registered his disapproval because she quickly went on. "But my birthday's not the real issue. It just helped me confirm what's been on my mind for a long time. The issue is that I want a baby."

Brick thumbed another tablet from the roll and popped it into his mouth. "Thirty's still young."

"I know, but I don't want to wait until I'm thirty-five or forty and feeling desperate." Lisa pushed back her hair. "It's hard to explain, Brick. I just have this strong, strong feeling that now is when I want to have a baby."

There was dead silence except for him crunching the tablet between his teeth. Brick felt Lisa's expectant gaze on him. *Marriage.* His stomach twisted violently. "I'm not ready."

Another dead silence followed his words. She squared her shoulders. "That's what I thought," she managed in a quiet, unsteady voice.

Appearing to brace herself, she took a deep breath and gave a tremulous smile. "It wouldn't be fair for me to try to badger you into changing your mind, and I wouldn't be happy staying in this"— she waved her hand searchingly—"non-relationship. So we can't keep—" Her voice broke off, and she took a few seconds to get back on track.

"I can't tell you how much these last months have meant to me. Being with you has made me more confident. I need to thank you for that and for everything you've taught me about myself." She looked away self-consciously. "And for everything you've taught me about men."

Everything you've taught me about men! Reeling from that last statement, Brick watched in utter disbelief as Lisa rose from the bed and quickly pulled on her robe. She set his clothes on the bed beside him. Lisa was talking, but he couldn't hear for the roar in his ears.

He got out of bed and planted himself directly in front of her. "You're dumping me!"

Lisa blinked. "I wouldn't really call it dumping." Her gaze slid away from him. "Would you please get dressed?"

Frustration bucked through him. "What's the matter? You don't like my body anymore?"

Lisa shot him a dark look. "I never said I didn't like your body. It's just distracting for you to stand there stark naked when we're trying to talk."

Brick saw the resolute expression on her face and swore. In heated silence, he jerked on his jeans and shirt. "If you wouldn't call it dumping, then what would you call it?"

Lisa sighed. "We want different things. I want family and commitment. You want a good time. It's stupid for us to continue to want things from each other that we just can't give. I've been reading some books on the subject, and—"

Brick groaned and sat down on the bed to pull on his shoes. Not another one of those women's self-help books. They would be the death of him yet.

"—they say it's better if you make a clean break in this case. It has taken me two months to be able to do it, but I think it's for the best." Her voice wavered as if she were fighting back tears.

Brick was dealing with a surprisingly sharp pain in his chest. He stood. "So this is it?" he asked, still not quite able to comprehend it. "After nine months of being together, this is it."

Lisa closed her eyes, appearing to gather her composure. "I guess it is," she finally said in a small voice as she opened her eyes. "I wish—" She pressed her lips together and shook her head as if she'd made a vow not to make any more wishes concerning him.

With every passing second, she seemed to grow farther and farther away from him. She'd taken him by surprise, and he was left not knowing what to do. He'd been completely faithful to her and as thoughtful as he knew how to be. He'd also, however, assumed he had the upper hand in their relationship and always evaded any discussion about commitment. He was battling confusion at the same time he realized that she meant what she was saying. She meant to end it, and he wasn't ready for that either. He plowed his fingers through his hair, not knowing what the hell to do or say. "Can I kiss you?"

Wrapping her arms around herself, Lisa took a step back. She shook her head again. "I don't think it would be a good idea."

Her refusal cut like a knife. "Then why'd you go—" He gestured toward the bed.

"I-I hadn't really intended to, but you—"

"But I was ready and raring to go the second I saw you. Like I always am," he finished in disgust, recalling her slight hesitation when he'd kissed the breath out of her and carried her to bed. Feeling lost, he shoved his hands in his pockets. "I guess this is good-bye."

Lisa's eyes welled with tears. "I guess it is," she whispered.

Brick walked to the front door and put his hand on the cold doorknob. He hesitated. This was nuts. Maybe they could talk about it some more. Maybe Lisa could wait a little longer. Wait for what? his conscience chided. He was never going to get married and have children. Something inside him rebelled at the thought of not being with her anymore, though. Having no idea what he could say, he turned. "Lisa?"

"Go on," Lisa urged. Her body was more shadow than substance in the dark hallway, but her voice was sure. "You've already said good-bye."

With a bitter taste in his mouth, Brick opened the door and walked out.

Lisa didn't breathe until she heard his footsteps completely fade away. Panic squeezed her chest like a huge rubber band, and she breathed so quickly, she feared she might hyperventilate. She grabbed a paper bag from a cabinet beneath the kitchen sink and yanked it over her head. She concentrated on breathing slowly and deeply.

Lord help her, she'd done it. After two months of rehearsing and letting futile wishes die, she'd ended her relationship with Brick Pendleton.

It would be easier to dismiss Brick if he were shallow or cruel, but Lisa knew better. He'd been fair and square with her from the beginning. Marriage wasn't in his plans, he'd told her, and she'd accepted his stand until her feelings had grown to where she couldn't conceal them. She knew Brick had been promoted to a division director in his business because of his hard work, honesty, and fairness. He had the respect of not only his profession, but the whole community.

He was a man of action and compassion. When the Midwest had suffered from horrible floods, he'd organized a relief program that had benefited the flood victims and the citizens of Chattanooga who'd watched the devastation on the news every night and felt helpless.

He'd been a passionate and thoughtful lover. He always held her after they made love, and there'd been a few times she sensed the holding had been as much for him as it had been for her.

And she'd just told him good-bye.

"It's the right thing to do," she repeated to herself for the two hundredth time, and pulled the bag from her head.

She turned off the lights and went back to her bedroom. The bed was a tumbled mess, and the air seemed to mock her with his scent. Ignoring the quick clutch in her heart, Lisa stripped the bed and immediately tossed the sheets into the washer. She sprayed air freshener until she nearly choked from the "fresh spring" scent.

Lisa would be the first to admit she'd never been comfortable around men. Since she was a child, she'd always been the tallest girl in the class, and she hadn't carried her height gracefully until a few years before when she'd stopped trying so hard to figure out how to attract men. Ironically, at the same time it seemed men had begun to notice her, but Lisa had plunged herself into making her catering business a success. Except for an occasional date, she focused her time and energy on her career. It was something she found she had a measure of control over, and that gave her the biggest rush she'd ever experienced.

Until Brick. When she'd first started dating him, one of her friends had warned her that she was playing with dynamite. Lisa had laughed and assumed the woman was making a little pun since Brick was an expert in demolition. Now, however, she knew the truth. Brick had turned her life upside down. He'd made her acutely aware of her femininity, her sexuality, and, ultimately, her womanhood. Although he would be horrified to know it, he was responsible for bringing the desire for hearth and home to the surface.

For years Lisa had buried her secret wishes and desires beneath a more practical facade, but now she could no longer ignore the wishes of the real Lisa. The real Lisa had the audacity to want a man to share her life with, and a baby. According to five books she'd read in the last few months, there was no reason she couldn't have what she wanted. It just took a little strategy and a lot of practicality, starting with the end of her non-relationship with Brick.

She looked at the sets of sheets in her linen closet and felt a strange tug. Brick had made love to her on every single set except one. Desperately fighting back a wave of melancholy, she unwrapped the brand-new sheets and put them on her queen-size bed. She took a shower in an attempt to delete the memory of his most recent possession of her.

Her teeth brushed and hair dried, Lisa turned off the light and slipped beneath the covers. The sheets were crisp to the point of scratchy. Her head ached from the too-sweet scent of the air freshener. Her eyes burned from holding back tears. Her stomach felt sick with regret. And her heart, oh Lord, her heart just plain hurt.

Suddenly, it was too much. She closed her eyes against hot tears spilling down her cheeks. Her body jerked from a broken sob. She'd known it was going to hurt, but she'd never dreamed she'd feel ripped apart. All her spraying and washing might get rid of Brick on the outside. But how, she wondered, could she get rid of him on the inside?

Three weeks later, Lisa went out with Mark, a nice, quiet tax attorney who would probably make someone a fine husband. Although she didn't feel the faintest spark of attraction toward him, Lisa was determined to keep an open mind. After seeing a movie, they went to the bar where she'd first met Brick. She was uneasy from the moment she set foot in the place. She'd done her best to avoid Brick and the places they'd frequented.

Her skin buzzing with trepidation, she ordered

a Marguerita to calm her nerves. An odd mix of disappointment and relief fell over her when she didn't see Brick, and she made idle conversation with the oh-so-serious tax attorney. Spotting a business associate, her date excused himself. In his absence, Lisa stared at the table and easily recalled the dozens of reasons why she'd always hated first dates.

"How've you been, Lisa?"

The low, husky voice jerked her attention away from the tabletop. Lisa stared at Brick, taking in his tousled brown hair and questioning eyes.

The memory of the first moment they'd met hit her like a cyclone. He carried his size with masculine ease. That was the first thing that had impressed her. She'd had a difficult time keeping her gaze off of him as he stood across the room at the bar. And she'd been shocked when he'd looked back. Not surprisingly, there'd been a woman standing beside him trying to get his attention. He'd been distantly polite while he finished his bottle of beer and kept his gaze trained on Lisa.

Lisa had grown so uncomfortable that she'd deliberately looked away and thought about making her excuses to her friends and leaving. When he'd showed up beside her table with a smile that said, "I'm harmless," and violet eyes that said, "You're mine," it was all she could do to breathe, let alone speak.

Tonight, the violet eyes said the same thing, but there was no playful, harmless grin. She didn't know if it was fear, passion, or insanity, but her pulse skipped into double time.

He wore a white shirt open at the neck, the sleeves casually folded up. The light color emphasized his tan and brought her attention to his throat where, she'd learned, he was a little ticklish. They used to play a game where she nuzzled his neck with kisses and he would try not to laugh. She allowed her gaze to fall to his strong forearms. How many times had he lifted her and carried her as if she weighed no more than a child?

Not anymore.

Lisa sucked in a quick breath and felt the cork pop on all the emotions she'd stuffed down inside her. For one horrifying moment, she felt the strangest urge to cry.

Appalled at the thought, she swallowed hard, cleared her throat, and recalled that he'd asked her a question. "I've been fine," she managed. "And you?"

He shrugged. "Busy at work. I called you a few times and got your answering machine." He hooked his foot on the platform where her table was located and leaned closer.

His position cut off the rest of the room and somehow made their conversation seem more intimate. Lisa shifted slightly away. "Yes, well—"

"My sister owns a riverboat down in Beulah County. She's having a get-together for my six brothers, and I'd like you to come."

"I didn't know you had a sister and six brothers," she said, dismayed that the small piece of personal information should affect her so.

"I guess I never got around to telling you. Would it have mattered?"

Would it have? Lisa faltered. She'd always sensed Brick kept his life strictly divided into different areas that rarely overlapped. He'd shared a little about his job with her, but nothing about his family. That had hurt. It had been one more piece of evidence that he wasn't serious about her. "I don't know."

"Listen, Lisa, I've been thinking. A lot." He put his hand over hers and stared intently into her eyes. His voice deepened. "I've been missing you a lot too."

Lisa's heart pounded against her rib cage.

"We had something damn good, and it seems like it was over in less than a minute. We called it off without looking at the possibilities."

Lisa could feel herself sinking under his spell again, and she knew what would happen if she did. Just the touch of his hand made her tremble, and the look in his eyes could melt steel. If she followed her heart, she'd end up in bed with him within thirty minutes. It would be incredible sex. Her breasts tightened at the mere thought of it. After it was over, however, Brick would stall any deep discussions, and she'd feel emotionally frustrated.

"I don't think—" She broke off, feeling both relieved and uneasy when she spotted Mark on his way back to the table. "There's my date."

Brick's gaze widened. "Date?"

Lisa pasted a smile on her face and eased her hand from Brick's. "Mark Lawford, this is Brick Pendleton. He's a—a—"

Both men gazed at her expectantly.

"He's a demolition expert," she finished weakly.

Brick stared at Lisa in disbelief.

"Well, how about that," Mark said, extending his hand. "You blow up buildings for a living?"

Brick tore his gaze away from Lisa and shook Mark's hand. "Not really. I used to do more work blasting foundations," he said, still blindsided by how Lisa had described him. Demolition expert. Not ex-lover, friend, or the man who knew every inch of her body. He took a slow, deep breath. Brick prided himself on his great sense of humor, but his grin felt a little forced by the time he got to it. "I only use explosives every now and then. Most of my work is done with machinery."

"That must be something. Hey, you want to join us? I'll buy you a drink, and you can tell us some of your war stories."

Brick slid a glance over to Lisa. She gave a quick, desperate shake of her head. He hesitated. If he were a nice, polite guy, he'd excuse himself, but he wasn't feeling particularly polite right now. He slid into a chair directly opposite Lisa. "Sounds good to me. I'll take a beer and tell you as many stories as you want."

Over the next hour, Brick shared a few tales with Mark and Lisa. He noticed that Lisa avoided his gaze, and every time she did, he struggled with the perverse urge to do something to get her attention. Brick couldn't see Lisa getting serious about Mark, but, then, he couldn't see Lisa getting serious about anyone but himself. And he refused to consider the prospect of another man in her bed.

He shifted slightly and his knee bumped hers. She drew back and dodged his gaze again. Brick felt a lick of impatience and sipped his beer. "So what movie did y'all go see?"

Mark named an action flick, and Lisa toyed with her watch. She was doing her best to ignore him, and Brick was tired of being ignored. "Did you close your eyes during the shoot-out scenes?" he gently teased her.

If he'd been sitting beside her, he would have squeezed her waist. Instead, he extended his feet on either side of hers and put them just close enough to make her aware of him. Her startled gaze finally shot up to meet his.

Lisa struggled to disentangle her bare legs from his. The brush of denim and the strength and warmth of his knees capturing hers sent a chaotic heat pulsing through her bloodstream. "I kept my eyes open except for two times," she admitted, glaring at him when she freed her legs.

Mark glanced from Brick to Lisa quizzically. "You never told me how you two met."

Trying to salvage what she could of this disastrous date, Lisa forced a smile and said casually, "As a matter of fact, we met here about nine months ago." She shot Brick a warning look.

Brick's eyes glinted dangerously. "Nine months and twenty-three days," he corrected. "And that was just the beginning."

TWO

"He's kinda scrawny," Brick said forty-five minutes later when Lisa jerked open her door.

"Everyone looks scrawny to you," she retorted, completely exasperated. Back at the bar Mark Lawford had picked up on Brick's tone and looked at Lisa with questions just waiting to be asked. Lisa had been so embarrassed, she didn't have a prayer of forming an adequate response. She wasn't pleased with the sense of relief she'd felt when Mark hadn't kissed her good night. She wasn't pleased that her first date "with a goal" had ended so disastrously. And she wasn't pleased that she didn't know who she was more angry with, Brick or herself.

She would never have let him in except that he claimed to have her address book, and when she'd checked her purse, sure enough, she'd found it missing. Her address book was one of the keys to her search for a husband. In the wrong hands, the information it contained would be humiliating. Lisa held out her hand. "Where's my address book?"

"In a minute," he promised. "Let's have a drink and a little conversation first." He strolled past her into the small den.

Lisa's grip tightened on the door, and she closed her eyes in frustration. She'd done pretty well in her quest to get past Brick and start looking for the future father of her children, until she'd run into her former lover. *Former lover.* The thought caused her stomach to tighten.

Lisa slammed the door mentally and physically. Determined to get rid of Brick, she whipped around and went into the den. "I'm not going to offer you a drink," she said through gritted teeth to the man who lounged on her sofa. "I'm going to ask for my address book, thank you, escort you to the door, and say good night. That's the program. Got it?"

Brick locked gazes with her for a long moment. After seeming to measure her determination, he frowned and pulled the small paisley cloth-covered book from his pocket. He stood. "What are three stars for?"

Humiliation crowded her chest. Lisa felt her cheeks burn with heat. She snatched the book from his hand. "It's nothing you need to worry about."

"Oh, but I do worry about you." Brick took a step closer and looked down at her. "I wonder if you're trying to cater too many parties. I wonder if you're forgetting to eat dinner. I wonder if you're working so hard that you forget to have fun."

Lisa tried not to let his concern soften her resolve. "I ate dinner tonight, and I *was* having fun with Mark."

Based on his expression of disbelief, Brick must have guessed that last comment was a stretch, but he let it pass. "I wonder if you've backed into something this week."

Lisa pressed her lips together. The man knew entirely too much about her, even her little problem with backing into things with her car. Just that morning she'd barely missed a mailbox. "Not a thing."

He paused and his face was utterly sincere. "Ever since you kicked me out of your apartment after making love to me like a wild woman—"

The reminder murmured in his low, husky voice singed her from head to toe. Taking a deep breath, Lisa stepped back. "I did not kick you out. It wasn't as if we lived together or anything."

He moved closer and lifted a strand of her hair. "Then what would you call it?"

"I—I—" She swallowed over her fumbling tongue. His nearness affected her as if she'd risen too fast after deep-sea diving. His gaze roamed over her from head to toe. He wanted to touch her everywhere he'd looked, she realized. Her body melted. "I invited you to leave," she managed in a strained voice.

He lifted an eyebrow and twined his fingers through her hair. "Next time," he said quietly, "I guess I'll have to turn down that invitation."

His thumb grazed the soft curve of her jaw, and Lisa had to resist the urge to turn her face into his wide palm. "Next time I won't invite. Next time I'll—"

He pressed his thumb over her lips, halting her threat. "I've missed you."

She drew a shaky breath. His simple direct words had the impact of a bomb detonating inside her.

"I've missed holding you, kissing you, making love to you. And I've missed talking to you." He lowered his head closer to hers so that she didn't just hear his words, she felt them. He dropped his thumb from her mouth and curled his hand around her waist. "Tell the truth, Lisa. Haven't you missed me just a little bit?"

Lisa experienced a rush of emotion inside her so intense that it hurt to look at him. She squished her eyes closed. "Oh, Brick," she whispered.

His warm mouth captured hers, his tongue slid gently past her lips, and Lisa's knees and resolve dipped. It was an I-don't-want-to-do-without-you kiss packed with tender seduction. Her hands groped for his shoulders, and she was immediately enveloped in his arms.

With his hand at the small of her back, he matched their lower bodies together so that she felt him intimately against her abdomen. Lisa's heart nearly burst. She'd missed him in this way too. Missed his arms around her, missed his hungry kiss, and missed the way he openly showed his need for her, a need he wanted *her* to satisfy.

Undiluted arousal surged through her like straight whiskey, robbing her breath and sanity. Her thighs tingled, a restless ache settled low in her belly, and instinctively she wanted to touch him where he grew taut and hard. He'd always liked it when she touched him. She skimmed her hand down his chest to his belly.

He gave an encouraging groan that vibrated deliciously through her mouth. She slipped her fingers closer to the very edge of his straining masculinity.

He shifted his pelvis toward her hand and pulled his mouth from hers. His head dipped toward her shoulder, and his uneven breaths matched hers. "God, I've missed you, Lisa. It's been too long. Let me take you to bed."

The word *bed* slapped at Lisa like two cymbals crashing against each other, reverberating throughout her overheated consciousness.

One of his hands rose to caress her breast, and she felt another sensual tug inside her. "Lisa," he muttered, pressing his erection into her hand again, seeking her intimate touch.

Her mind and body were in total disagreement about what she should do next.

What was she doing? her conscience screamed. Lisa pulled back her hand and pushed against his shoulder. Three weeks away from him, one kiss, and she'd lost it. "Oh, Lord, what am I doing?" she whispered brokenly, turning away from him and immediately missing his warmth. She wrapped her arms around her waist.

Brick's body rebelled at the sudden distance between them. He reached for her, but she jerked away from him. His hands felt empty beyond belief. *What had happened?* One minute she was the epitome of feminine heat in his arms, the next, she'd pulled away. Brick shook his head to clear it. She sounded almost as if she were crying. The notion nearly tore him in two. Wanting to hold her, needing to hold her, he touched her arm.

"No!" Lisa nearly jumped out of her skin. She pushed back her hair. "I don't want—" She swallowed and shook her head. "I don't want this. I didn't want this."

Brick paused, absorbing the quick hurt. "Yes, you did. We both did."

"Okay," she admitted. "My body did." She took a deep breath and finally met his gaze. "But my brain didn't. This—whatever it is between us." She waved her hands in exasperation. "It's useless. I tried to tell you before."

Brick plowed his fingers through his hair. "It didn't feel useless to me. Making love with you has always been more than—"

"That isn't what I meant." Her eyes darkened. "It was exciting. It's always exciting, but after it's over . . ." Lisa sighed and her explanation faded out.

"After it's over, what happens?" he asked, feeling a sting of remorse. Had he been so inconsiderate that he'd foregone her pleasure for his? Lord knew, when he made love to Lisa, he had the sensation of a five-alarm fire that had to be put out, but her pleasure had always been important to him.

"After it's over," she began, and hesitated again. "You're still you, and I'm still me. You still want no strings, and I still want a family. You usually go home, and the next morning I feel . . ." She shrugged. "Empty."

Brick was the first to admit that the feminine psyche was a complete mystery to him. "Is this about me staying overnight? Because if it is—"

"It's about you staying every night."

Brick felt a muscle spasm in his jaw. Uneasiness grabbed and clutched at his gut. He shoved his clenched hand into his pocket. Hell, he simply was not ready to cut Lisa loose. He didn't want to give her up yet. When he'd seen that little book of hers with his name crossed out, he'd felt undiluted panic. "We could live together."

Her eyes rounded in surprise. Uncertainty flashed across her face, but only for a second. Lisa looked away. "I don't think so," she said quietly.

"Lisa, maybe this is just a stage," he said, voicing what he'd been hoping because he couldn't accept not being with her anymore. "Look at how wrapped up in your job you've been. Now, all of a sudden, you want marriage and a baby. Maybe this will all blow over in a couple of weeks or a month."

"It's not all of a sudden," she wailed. "And I don't expect you to understand because I don't think you really know me that well."

Affronted, Brick stared at her in disbelief. "What the hell—"

Lisa held up a hand. "You know me sexually, but not in other ways. The other ways a woman wants to be known by a man."

With a sinking sensation, Brick sensed her resolve. It was something new, and he hadn't come to grips with it. Before, she'd always been flexible, almost malleable, and he'd hoped he'd be able to talk her around this latest glitch the way he'd always done before. But she looked as if she'd faced something inside herself and come out stronger because of it.

Even though he topped her by five inches and outweighed her by a hundred pounds, Brick, who was known for his power, found himself envying her strength.

Lisa had made a decision grounded in what she thought was best. What she'd decided, he realized, was that she didn't want him.

Brick pulled off the handkerchief he'd tied around his head to keep the sweat from his eyes and accepted the chair and cold beer his sister Carly offered. "Thanks."

His brother-in-law Russ Bradford took another chair and saluted Brick with his own beer. "Appreciate your help. When you said you were coming down for the weekend, I swear I wasn't planning to work you to death."

"I'm a long way from dying," Brick said, though he felt miserable inside. He knew Russ needed help, and Brick needed something to quell the restlessness within him. So far, he hadn't found it. "Since I've been here so often lately, I thought I'd better earn my keep."

"It's no problem and you know it," Carly said. "Are you sure you don't want to come along for the dinner cruise on *Matilda's Dream*? I could make space for you." She grinned. "After all, you used to be part owner."

"One of eight owners," he said wryly. Brick's six brothers, he, and Carly had inherited the riverboat from an aunt. Russ had bought out the brothers' shares and Carly had taken it over and made it into a successful business.

Brick wasn't in the mood to socialize. If he were honest with himself, he wasn't in the mood for much of anything. "Thanks for the offer, but I think I'll stay here tonight."

Carly frowned in concern. "Business okay?"

"Booming," Brick said.

She exchanged a sidelong glance with Russ. "Anything else bothering you?"

Brick shrugged. "Nothing that a few more beers and a shower won't cure."

"What's her name?" Russ asked.

Brick stopped midmotion in lifting the can to his lips, then set it down on the table. He didn't look at Carly or Russ. He knew what he would see. Russ would be wearing that probing, no-nonsense, give-me-some-answers expression, and Carly would look worried. And Brick had thought he'd fooled them all. "It's no big deal. It's all over, anyway."

"If it's no big deal, then why have you been here five of the last six weekends?"

That stung. Brick tried to shake it off and forced a grin. "Hey, if I've been imposing, you should let me know. I'm sleeping all the way over on the opposite side of the house, so I've only heard you scream once or twice."

His younger sister didn't blush. She rolled her eyes. "I knew we wouldn't get a straight answer from you. The CIA could take lessons from you on how to keep from disclosing secrets. You must not have been too serious about her, or you would have brought her down here for us to meet."

Brick rubbed his finger in the condensation on the can. "Why would I do that?"

She looked at him with ill-concealed impatience. "Because that's the normal thing to do. When you really care about a woman, you want her to meet your adorable younger sister and all six of your brothers. You don't just want her to meet them. You want her to like them."

"Yeah, well, maybe she didn't want to meet my family."

Silence hung heavy in the room, and Brick looked up to meet his sister's gaze. "And maybe I waited until it was too late."

The next day Brick returned to Chattanooga with Russ's words ringing in his ears, "Too late is when she's got somebody else's wedding band on her finger."

He hadn't ever spent much time thinking about why he didn't want to get married, because it was one of those things that he had decided when he was twelve years old. His mother had died, and his father might as well have. For the sake of the kids he'd remarried a sour woman who'd grown more sour because his father couldn't love her.

Carly had spent a year stuttering, his oldest brother, Daniel, had become an old man before his time. His stepmother had nearly ruined Garth. Brick had watched his family flounder, and in the middle of it all, he had felt lost.

His mother had been the silken thread of joy that had bound them all together. He'd been angry that she'd left them. His anger had turned to fear when he watched what her death did to his father. All this, Brick realized, because his father had loved his mother too much. It was a knowledge that seemed to spring from his very soul.

At the idea of marriage, Brick experienced a physical and visceral response. His skin grew clammy, his mouth went dry, and he felt as if he were going to throw up. Even now, as he drove into Chattanooga, he felt it, the powerful edginess that went beyond simple aversion. In the past he'd always put it down to exceptional male survival instincts.

Since two of his brothers and his sister Carly had taken the plunge and gotten married, though, he was forced to reevaluate. Daniel had been acting like a kid out of school since he'd married Sara Kingston a few months earlier. Brick never would have believed it, but since Garth had hooked Erin Lindsey, he was happier than Brick could have imagined. And Carly seemed utterly content in her marriage to Russ.

But Brick thought of a friend who worked in construction. The guy used to work the high beams until one day when he fell. After that, Brick's friend told him that even the thought of going up again made him break into a cold sweat.

For a sliver of a moment, Brick wondered if a man could develop the same clinical kind of fear of marriage. Uneasiness trickled in. Brick snorted in disbelief. A phobia about marriage? *Get real.* What would they call it?

Ten minutes later, he was cruising the parking lot of Lisa's apartment complex. After noting that her car was there, he parked and rang her doorbell. It was a warm day, so he decided to check the pool too. He knew Lisa usually took a break from working on Sunday afternoon.

She was stretched out on a chaise lounge, slathering sunscreen all over her nearly bare body. Her hair was loosely piled on top of her head, and a huge pair of sunglasses with white frames was sliding down her nose. She wore a purple one-piece bathing suit with flowers all over it and skinny little straps holding up the delectably filled bodice. It was cut low enough in front and high enough on the thighs that Brick could have used some aspirin to bring down the sudden surge of his body temperature. His mouth watered just looking at her. Didn't women realize that one of most men's top ten fantasies usually involved taking off a woman's bathing suit, lathering her down with something slippery, then having her return the favor to him?

He dipped his hand into the pool, splashed some water on his face, and walked toward her. He shook his head. One look, he thought, and she'd turned him inside out.

"Need some help," he offered.

Lisa's head whipped around.

He saw a spark of recognition and excitement flicker through her eyes just before she shoved the glasses back into place. Hoping like hell he didn't screw up, he pulled a chair closer and sat down.

"No. I'm about done." She smoothed the cream over her shoulders one last time.

Brick noticed a dot of unspread lotion on the inside of her left breast and felt a ridiculous envy for her suntan lotion. He hadn't touched her intimately in over a month. "You missed a spot."

Lisa glanced down the front of her, her sunglasses slipping again. "Where?"

Brick lowered his voice. "Where you used to let me touch you."

Lisa went completely still. Her gaze automatically went to her thighs, and then to Brick. A memory taunted her of his hands caressing and teasing her until she arched against him, and his hard legs brushing against her softer ones as he slowly slid inside her . . . With devastating speed, she felt the beginning of her body's automatic response. She bit the inside of her cheek. Edgy, she sucked in a deep breath and crammed her sunglasses back up again. "Oh for Pete's sake! Where is it?"

Before she could blink, he put one index finger on her breast and gently spread the dot of lotion. One second, she felt the sensuous stroke of his finger and was struck by the fascination his heavy-lidded gaze didn't hide. Then his hand was gone, and she was trying to get her brain to work.

"I wouldn't want you to get burned."

Lisa cleared her throat. She pushed down the cap on the lotion and tossed it into her tote bag. "No, I, uh, wouldn't—what are you doing here?"

He shrugged. "Just got back from Beulah County and thought I'd see how your—" He paused, wondering what to call it. "—search is going?"

She eased back into her chair and closed her eyes. Perhaps if she didn't look at him, her heart rate would settle down. "It's going fine. I have a date tonight."

"Is this a three-star man?"

Lisa refused to feel embarrassed about that again. "Of course."

"You never told me what three stars means."

"That's right. It's none of your business," she said cheerfully.

"Must be damned convenient to be able to turn your feelings on and off like a faucet," he said sincerely. "I haven't had the same luck."

Lisa blinked and stared at him. His words shook her. "Oh, for crying out loud, I never—"

"Just because you're gonna marry another man," Brick said the words, and felt as if he were chewing nails, "doesn't mean we can't be friends, does it?"

The sudden look of confusion on Lisa's face would have been amusing if Brick hadn't been fighting for his life. "Friends?" she said tentatively, as if it were a new word.

"Sure. It's a lot better than being enemies." *It's a lot better than nothing*, he added to himself.

"We've never really been *friends*," Lisa said, her voice laced in skepticism.

Brick had to work to take that jab in stride. "With all your . . . dates"—Brick forced the repugnant word out—"it would be nice to have a friend around, someone you've known for a long time, someone who knows you, someone you don't have to impress." He grinned. "Someone you could tell what those three stars represent."

Lisa laughed uncertainly and shook her head. "You're crazy."

"C'mon," Brick said, putting a little dare in his voice. "If I were your friend, you'd tell me, wouldn't you?"

Lisa hesitated, looking doubtful. She cocked her head to one side, and Brick wished he could take off her sunglasses to read her eyes. She gave a sigh. "All right. The three stars mean the man likes women and children, and he's not opposed to the general idea of marriage."

"What about money, appearance, age, and sex?"

Lisa gave a little shrug. "They're all secondary to the other three qualities. Age and appearance can be settled on the first date, money by the second, and sex . . ."

Brick's gut tightened.

"Sex would be last."

Sex with another man would be never, if Brick had anything to do with it. He rubbed his hand over his mouth in restraint. "It sounds like a plan," he muttered.

"It is. This book I've been reading says you can get married in less than two years. It talks about keeping a practical attitude and using your resources."

The book again. "Using your resources?"

Lisa nodded. "One of the most interesting facts it reported was that many married couples are introduced by mutual friends, so the author suggested that you tell all your friends that you're looking and ask for recommendations."

Lisa looked at him and a strange expression crossed her face. Brick experienced an even stranger foreboding. In the back of his mind he could almost hear the cock of a gun. She leaned forward, and her sunglasses slipped again to give him a view of the complete sincerity in her eyes. Her lips curved into a slow, siren smile designed to drop a man at fifty paces. And Brick was at one and a half.

"Tell me, Brick," she said sweetly, "can you recommend one of your friends to father my children?"

THREE

She might as well have shot him.

Speechless, Brick stared at her for a full minute.

"Did you hear what I said?" Lisa asked. "I asked you if—"

"I heard you," he finally managed, thinking he could use a double Jack Daniels straight up right now. Where had that breeze gone? he wondered as he tugged on his collar. "I'll have to think about it and get back to you. I don't usually evaluate my friends with an eye as to how good they'd be at fathering children."

"I guess not," she conceded, and spritzed her neck with a spray bottle of water.

His gaze honed in on the droplets dotting her chest. He wanted to lick every bit of water from her skin, spritz her, and do it again until his thirst was at least temporarily quenched. Instead he licked his lips and turned to the pool where a couple of kids played splashing games. "It sounds as if you've got this all planned out."

"Some of it." Lisa pulled a sheet of paper from her tote bag. "I got this in the mail the other day."

Brick leaned forward to read it. "Meet your mate, not just a date. A dating service?" he said, unable to hide his horror. "Have you gone crazy? You'll have every nut in Tennessee calling you day and night."

She set her chin stubbornly. "It's just one of my options. Senada's also—"

"Senada!"

When Lisa's chin rose another notch, Brick bit his tongue, laced his fingers together, and cracked all his knuckles at once.

"She knows a lot of men."

"That's putting it mildly," he muttered.

"She knows a lot more about men than I do and—"

"—You always knew enough for me," he pointed out in a dark velvet voice. "And what you didn't know, I sure as hell liked teaching you."

Lisa's heart seemed to pause, then flutter wildly. She'd kept the conversation centered on her search for a husband as a means of protection because she felt more than bare beneath Brick's gaze. She felt naked.

Every time his eyes lingered, she felt as if he'd touched her. Could he tell she was having a hard time breathing normally? Could he sense the way her nipples tingled? Did he know about the insidious moist warmth that built within her because her body simply couldn't forget what he'd been to her? He was looking at her as if she were the only woman in the world, and despite all her resolutions her mouth was cotton-dry from his intoxicating effect on her.

Lisa swallowed hard. "You don't understand. Senada's had a lot more experience—"

"I know," he said dryly.

"No." She sighed. "Let me put it this way. Senada was the kind of girl who had five offers to go to her high school prom."

"And?" Brick was waiting for the rest of the story. Something told him it would be important.

"And I got no offers," Lisa admitted reluctantly. "I was in the National Honor Society, I took piano lessons, went to church like a good girl. I was great with books, but when it came to guys, I was . . ."

"Shy," Brick supplied for her, feeling a twist of compassion. He recalled a few girls from his own high school days that had seemed awkward and shy with the boys. They'd often been the last ones picked for dates because their uneasiness had transferred itself to the boys.

She gave a small dip of her head. "That would be putting it very generously."

"You're not in high school anymore, Lisa."

"I know," she said softly. "I'm all grown up with a woman's body and mind—and a woman's needs." She gave a rueful smile. "But I've still got the heart of a child, and Senada tells me I've got plenty to offer the right man. I just need to find him."

Brick felt as if she'd just sliced him in two. He narrowed his eyes at the sharp pain. There was too much he hadn't told Lisa. In his quest to remain uncommitted, he'd managed to be blind as a bat about her vulnerabilities. She was a gentle woman, beautiful both inside and out, and if he'd had his act together, maybe she wouldn't be wondering if she would find the right man. If he'd had his head on straight, she'd be in his arms and he wouldn't feel like someone had ripped out his guts.

Brick took the first step in a new direction. He tugged off her glasses, hooked his thumb under her chin, and looked directly in her eyes. "You are so beautiful," he said, hearing the roughness in his own voice, "there aren't words enough to tell you. No matter what happens, don't ever forget that." He squeezed her chin slightly when she would have looked away. "Ever."

A long moment passed, with the sound of kids

doing cannonballs off the diving board in the background. In some corner of his mind, he heard a mother scolding her child. At the moment none of it meant squat to Brick if Lisa didn't believe him.

She bit her lip, and her eyelids fluttered down. "I don't think I could forget it." Then as if she couldn't bear the intensity emanating from him anymore, she lifted her chin away and quickly slid out of the other side of the lounge chair. "I think I need to cool off."

Brick nodded and stood. His mind full and his heart heavy, he watched her ease into the water. The ironic realization sank deep into his gut that he had spent his professional life tearing down things, destroying them. He was an expert at it. Hell, he couldn't enter a building without looking for the weak spots and figuring out how to bring it down.

He watched Lisa, and the sting of longing inside him grew. If he really wanted Lisa, then for the first time in his life he was going to have to put something *back together* and make it stronger than before.

"So, was the latest one any good?" Senada asked as she propped herself on Lisa's desk and crossed her legs.

Lisa quickly moved her papers out of the way of her flamboyant partner. Senada Calhoun, who had inherited her long black hair, year-round tan, and large brown eyes from her Puerto Rican mother, had also inherited her Texan father's ability to flirt. Thus she attracted men with the same ease that most normal humans brushed their teeth. Answering to the nickname Sin, Senada laughed and had a good time, but she didn't take any of the lust-struck men seriously.

She had, however, begun to take a very personal interest in Lisa's quest to find a husband. Lisa grimaced at the memory of her latest date. "He was interesting," she said evasively.

Senada arched one dark eyebrow. "Interesting is a polite way of saying he was a loser."

Lisa straightened the papers. "I wouldn't really say he was a loser, but I don't think we would be a good match. He was attractive, but he might like women a little too much. A year ago he joined this new alternative lifestyle group where a man's spiritual value is measured by how many wives he has."

"You're too kind. The sleaze was already married," Senada concluded without surprise.

"No. He's hoping to marry six different women within the next year, though." Lisa shook her head, remembering the dismay she'd felt when he'd told her the benefits of multiple marriage partners. "I'm working at being flexible, but I draw the line at polygamy."

"What about the one on Thursday night?"

"He was nice. Five inches shorter than I am." Lisa looked away from the amusement flickering in Senada's eyes. "I realize appearances really shouldn't matter, but . . ."

Senada giggled. "You don't have to make excuses to me, *la chica*. Have you heard from Rock lately?"

Lisa smothered a laugh. "Brick. His name is Brick." Since she'd broken up with Brick, Senada continually confused his name. Lisa was beginning to think it was deliberate.

Senada shrugged. "Brick. Rock. They're both the same—hardheaded."

"He stopped by to see me on Sunday." Lisa caught the chiding expression on Senada's face and rushed to explain. "He said he wants to be friends." She still wasn't sure how she felt about that.

"Uh-huh," Senada said, her voice dripping disbelief. "You agreed, and all the while your little heart was going pitter-patter because you still—"

"I do not," Lisa interrupted, desperate not to hear the rest of that statement spoken aloud. "And my heart is supposed to be beating all the time. I'd be dead if it didn't."

Senada sighed. "You really seem to like that not-quite-civilized, ruler-of-his-own-destiny type." She narrowed her eyes and paused, then her lips tilted in a slow smile. "I think I may have the perfect man for you."

❖━━━━━━━❖

The perfect man was out of town for the next few weeks, so Lisa accepted a few other recommendations Senada made. Between the spring wedding receptions, rehearsal dinners, graduation parties, and dates with a purpose, though, Lisa felt burned out enough to accept an invitation from Brick to attend a fair in Beulah County.

She told herself it was to prove that they were indeed friends. The "lover" part of their relationship was passed, finished, completely done, never to be repeated. If she felt a twinge of regret at the thought, she ignored it. She also told herself she wasn't the least bit curious about Brick's family.

At the fair, however, she stared at the sight of all those Pendletons as they crowded outside Brick's car.

Four tall men of varying ages with dark hair and Brick's violet eyes stood with three women, two of whom appeared to be pregnant. When Lisa noticed the differences between Brick and his brothers, she saw that Brick was the tallest, his hair was slightly lighter, and he exhibited a subtle masculine power that translated to pure sex appeal.

The pull was so strong that even with all these people around she had to force her attention away from him. It took a moment, but Lisa recognized the feminine version of the Pendletons as the young, slim woman who was not pregnant.

Brick instinctively put his hand at Lisa's back as he made the introductions. "This is Lisa Ransom. She's—" What? *The woman who'd wrecked his mental health. The woman who'd left him because he couldn't make a commitment. The woman who was planning to marry anyone but him as soon as possible.* He began to sweat.

"I'm a friend," Lisa said, giving Brick a meaningful smile. "I'm glad to meet you."

He clenched his jaw briefly, then smiled and gestured with his hand. "Daniel and his wife, Sara."

Lisa shook hands as he continued. "Garth and Erin, Jarod, Troy, and Carly."

A little boy wiggled between Garth and Erin. "Hey, I'm a Pendleton now too!"

"That's right," Brick said with a chuckle. "This is Luke, Garth and Erin's son."

"Lucky them." Lisa took one look at the bright-eyed boy with a cowlick on the crown of his head and smudges on his chin, and she fell in love. "And it looks like more Pendletons are on the way, so I guess congratulations are in order. When are you due?"

"September for us," said Erin, patting her stomach.

"Ours is due in November," Daniel said, taking Sara's hand.

Lisa sensed the love that flowed between them and felt a twinge of envy. She brushed it aside, though, and focused on getting a fix on the different personalities of Brick's family. Daniel was extremely solicitous of his wife, Sara, but she supposed the same could be said of Garth and Erin. Jarod seemed to observe in silence, while Troy was loud.

"Are we overwhelming you?" Carly asked.

"Not really. When Brick told me how many brothers he had, I imagined six 'Bricks.'"

"Heaven help us all," Carly said, rolling her eyes.

Lisa laughed. "Now I see that one's taller, one's quiet, one cracks jokes."

"Well, if you forget any names, don't feel bad. Just ask me and I'll be glad to give you a prompt. The twins, Ethan and Nathan, live out of state, so you'll be spared remembering their names this time."

"You own the riverboat, don't you?"

Carly nodded. "My husband Russ and I do."

"Oh, I didn't realize you were married."

Carly hesitated and lowered her voice. "Brick hasn't told you very much about us, has he?"

Lisa felt another twinge of pain, despite a hundred silent reminders that she shouldn't because her romantic relationship with Brick was over. "He, uh, mentioned you a month or so ago and . . ."

"Yeah, well, he mentioned you to us the last several times he visited."

That stopped Lisa in her tracks. She glanced at Brick and found him gazing at her while his brother Troy was talking. For an instant, his eyes seemed to meld with hers. She felt a shudder inside her, like the first rumblings of an earthquake. His gaze was so determined. She shuddered again.

The corners of his mouth lifted in a slow, knowing smile that made her heart pound against her rib cage. Lisa absently pressed her hand against her chest to make her heart behave.

"If you decide to stay overnight, you're welcome at my house," Carly offered.

Lisa ripped her gaze from Brick's. "Oh no. That won't be necessary. I'm not—"

"And if you have any questions about Brick," Carly said with a mischievous grin, "I've known him for twenty-plus years."

Lisa was severely tempted. A dozen unanswered questions came to mind. She told herself it was normal. After all, she'd been involved with Brick for months, and there was so much she had wanted to know about him.

Before. Not now.

She stifled the urge to ask, and instead mustered a smile. "Thanks, but I think I'll pass this time."

Brick overheard Lisa's response and didn't know

whether to be disappointed or relieved. He fought the overwhelming instinct to stuff Lisa in his car and drive back to Chattanooga. It was tough to explain why, even to himself, but he thought it had something to do with wanting to keep her to himself.

Selfish as hell, he acknowledged, but it didn't change the way he felt. He didn't want anyone messing with his relationship with her. He snorted. Why should he worry about them making matters worse when he'd already made a mess of it himself?

Brick dismissed the disturbing thoughts and snagged Lisa's wrist. "C'mon. Let's go throw a pie for charity. My old junior high school principal is the target, and I owe him."

Lisa stumbled after him. "Owe him for what?"

"He stuck me in detention for my whole seventh grade year."

"And you didn't deserve it at all?"

Brick stopped and grinned sheepishly. "Maybe a little."

"How little?"

"It was just a few harmless pranks . . . involving a frog and the English teacher, a food fight in the cafeteria, and . . ." He hesitated and his smile faded slightly. "And the homework I didn't do."

"I can imagine the frog and the food fight, but my father would have killed me if I hadn't done my homework."

Brick looked away, squinting his eyes under the glare of the sun. "Yeah, well, my dad wasn't paying much attention, my mother had died, and my stepmother was a witch."

The breeze picked up a strand of his sun-lightened hair, and Lisa felt a clutch in her chest. "Sounds rough," she murmured.

He shrugged his wide shoulders. "You don't want to hear about that, so—"

"But I do," she said impulsively, then bit her tongue. "I mean, I enjoy hearing about your childhood. You haven't really talked about it much before."

He rubbed his thumb back and forth over her knuckles in a mesmerizing motion. "It wasn't all happy, Lisa, and the time you and I had together was happy and good. Being with you was too special. I didn't want to drag it down."

She felt that same clutch again and swallowed hard. "Now that we're friends," she said in an effort to remind both herself and him, "maybe you won't feel like you're dragging anything down."

He lifted an eyebrow and glanced meaningfully at her lips. "We'll see."

He tugged her toward the pie booth, and Lisa surreptitiously wiped her mouth with the back of her hand. It felt as if he'd put his mouth there, against hers.

"You wanna go first?" he asked as he paid the attendant a few bucks.

"I don't know." Lisa looked doubtfully at the principal's friendly face behind the cutout cardboard. "I was never good at throwing things, or catching them for that matter," she said under her breath.

"Then let me help you." Brick gave Lisa a pie and positioned himself directly behind her. He wrapped one hand around her waist and meshed the front of his body with the back of hers. His chest rubbed against her back, the heat of his belly nearly scorching her skin, and his masculinity was deliciously pressed against her buttocks.

Lisa nearly dropped the pie.

"Whoa!" Brick caught it and reinforced her grip on it with his hand.

He stood so close that his familiar scent and the thud of his heart seemed to invade her body. He had a musky scent that she associated with sex and satisfaction. It was the closest she'd come to this kind of intimacy in weeks, and Lord help her, her breasts were tightening beneath the knit shirt she wore.

"I'm not sure—" She tried for a normal tone.

"C'mon. Just throw it a little high."

Lisa closed her eyes and tossed it.

"Not close enough," he muttered. "Let's do it one more time."

She remembered when he'd said those same words to her right after making love. "Oh, no." She moaned.

"You can do it." He placed another pie in her hand. Her surroundings began to feel surreal. The principal taunted Brick, but it was Brick's voice and body that became her focal point.

"C'mon, baby. Just a little higher and a little harder," he coaxed.

She blinked at the sensations his voice evoked, but she felt her nether regions begin a slow, sweet swell. "Higher and harder," she murmured, and tossed the pie as hard as she could.

She hit the principal dead center, and the surrounding crowd screamed with glee. Brick squeezed her waist and quickly kissed the side of her neck. "You were great, Lisa."

He meant throwing the pie, but all Lisa could think about was that last time they'd made love.

"That's some *friend* you got there, Brick."

"Shut up, Troy," Brick said with a growl.

"Ooh, I'm *all shook up*. Have you told her you and Elvis share—"

"Shut up!"

Troy raised his hands in appeal and backed away. "Just asking."

Lisa didn't have a clue what their exchange was about, but Troy's first comment hit her like a bucket of cold water. She wiggled out of Brick's hold on her. Avoiding his gaze, she took a few sanity-inducing steps away from him. "Your turn to throw a pie."

She stood, taking a few moments to regain her equilibrium. Frowning, she admired Brick's well-muscled form. His body attracted her, but it was his inherent male magnetism that drove her to distraction. She didn't like how quickly or easily she'd lost her perspective.

When his pie hit the principal, Brick tossed his head and laughed. His vitality seemed to spill over onto her. She wanted to be immune to him. She didn't want this dizzy, desperate feeling he caused. She didn't want it and she didn't need it.

Brick pulled Lisa against him for a quick hug and felt her stiffen. She'd been so soft and pliant against him moments before that his body had begun to respond. He hoped nobody was studying the front of his cutoffs right now, or the swollen ridge behind his zipper would make a joke out of everything he'd suggested about being "friends" with Lisa.

She tugged her hand away from his when he tried to hold it. Brick sighed. "Don't pay any attention to Troy. He's always had a big mouth."

Lisa fiddled with her fingers then folded them in front of her. "He reminded me that you and I are friends. That's all," she added emphatically. "And I'm looking for a husband."

Brick's view of the day took a sour plunge. His stomach felt unsettled. He pulled an antacid out of his pocket and slipped it in his mouth. Lisa's head was averted so that her gaze didn't meet his. A brooding feeling settled over him. "That's right," he muttered impatiently. "I forgot to ask. Any proposals lately?"

Lisa's head whipped up. She narrowed her eyes as if she hadn't missed the hint of a sarcastic edge in his voice. He could practically feel the heat of her indignation. She straightened her shoulders and lifted her chin.

Lord help him, there was that chin again. He should have kept his attitude under wraps. "Hey, that was out of line. I—"

"As a matter of fact," she said, overriding his apology, "I have received a proposal for marriage. Not just one, but two."

FOUR

Lisa immediately regretted her words. It wasn't as if she had any intention of marrying either man who'd proposed to her, and she didn't want to have to elaborate on the motivations behind their proposals. Based on the expression on Brick's face, however, she was in for the third degree.

And she would rather eat dirt than give him the details.

She smiled brightly. "I want a hot dog. I smelled them the minute I walked into the park, and my mouth's been watering ever since." She turned away from Brick. "You think they're over—"

Brick snagged her arm. "Just one minute," he said in a quiet, lethal voice. "Don't you want to tell me the rest of the story on these proposals?"

Lisa's nerves jangled inside her like a bunch

of bells. "Not really. What I want is a hot dog," she said, relieved that she'd managed not to meet his gaze. "And cotton candy," she added for good measure.

Brick lowered his lips to her ear. "I thought since I was your friend you'd want to tell me your secrets."

Lisa felt a sensual shiver buck and shimmy down her spine. Brick already knew far too many of her secrets. It was too easy to want to lean into his strength, to turn her head and bury her face in his strong neck and breathe in the scent and sensation of him. Too easy, and she couldn't do it. Fighting the fine edge of desperation, she arched away from the lure of his mouth. "If you were my friend, you'd point me to the nearest hot-dog stand because you could see I'm about to starve to death."

Still holding her wrist, Brick narrowed his eyes. He wanted to press her. She could feel the desire to demand war with the struggle for restraint emanating from him. In an instant his gaze changed and he shifted his clasp so that his fingers twined around hers. For all they'd shared, the gesture felt incredibly intimate, almost as if he were claiming her.

"I wouldn't ever want to be accused of not meeting your needs, Lisa." His voice caused a deep visceral clench in her stomach. "Remember that."

Her heart fluttered in her throat. She swallowed hard, but couldn't manage the words to tell him to let go of her hand.

Eight hours later after a full day at Beulah County's fair, they were flying up the highway toward Chattanooga with the T-top down and the night breeze blowing over them. Lisa sighed. She was pleasantly tired. At a different time, she would have snuggled closer to Brick and he would have rested his hand on her knee.

That was another lifetime, she told herself, straightening in her seat. Better to focus on something else. "Your family is nice. I like them, but with all those boys I can't help wondering if you fought a lot when you were growing up."

Brick nodded. "My father let us knock each other around until we were teenagers. By then I guess he got tired of the furniture getting smashed." He paused. "He worked on me a little earlier since I was the biggest."

"Worked on you?"

"Yeah. I developed a nasty temper the year my mother got sick. I got sent home from school one day with a shiner." Brick grinned. "The other guy had two, but my dad wasn't amused. He didn't scream or yell, though. He just told me to get to work on the lower forty. It took the whole summer on the working end of a hoe before I got my temper under control. I haven't hit anyone since."

"Even Troy?" Lisa asked with a knowing smile.

Brick laughed. "Even Troy."

"You must get angry sometime. What do you do now?"

"Not often," Brick said, thinking, however, that he'd experienced some nearly uncontrollable frustration lately. He couldn't exactly explain that fact to Lisa if he wanted her to continue letting him be her friend. What a hell of a farce this was. He didn't want her trying out other men for husband material. He didn't want to stay away from her. He wanted her back. His eyes were focused on the road, but the sound of her voice and the every-now-and-then trace of her scent sent his libido into overdrive and his guts into a tangled mess.

Noticing that she was still waiting for him to respond, he shrugged. "I guess I do the usual things—count to ten, leave the room, crack my knuckles. And if it's really bad I—" He stopped, suddenly self-conscious.

Lisa leaned closer. "You what?"

"It's nothing. I just—"

"You just don't want to tell me," she finished, disappointment coloring her voice.

Aw hell. "Okay. I'll tell you one of my secrets if you tell me one of yours."

She paused only a fraction of a moment. "Deal."

"When I feel like I'm close to losing it, I whistle."

There was a long gap of silence, then Lisa smothered a giggle. "Whistle?"

Brick threw a quick glance at her and grinned despite the fact that the joke was at his expense. "Yeah. Go ahead and laugh. You look like you're about to bust."

Lisa let out a full-bodied, throaty laugh, the kind that made Brick's gut clench in memory.

"I'm just—" She coughed over another laugh. "I'm just trying to imagine how you do it." She cleared her throat. "And why?"

"Well, it takes a lot of concentration if you whistle something intricate."

"Okay. I'll buy that," she said, sinking down in the leather seat. "But you know, I don't think I've ever heard you whistle."

Brick thought for a long moment. "I guess I never got mad at you. I was too busy—" He stopped, unwilling to finish.

"Too busy?" she softly prompted.

Too busy falling in love. His heart stopped at the realization. Hell, he would have to deal with that later. "Too busy being happy," he said instead, and quickly changed the subject. "Time for the flip side of the deal. You gotta tell me one of your secrets."

Lisa shifted in her seat. "Do I get to pick?"

Brick shook his head. "I want to know who proposed."

Lisa groaned. "I should have seen this coming. It's no one you know. And I told both of them no."

"That's a relief," he muttered under his breath. "Who?"

She gave a long-suffering sigh. "One was this friend of a friend of a—"

"I get the picture," he said dryly.

"He's a nice insurance salesman. Very religious."

"And?" he persisted.

"And he wanted some wives. I believe he said six."

"Six!" Brick shook his head. He couldn't have heard correctly.

"Yes. Six. He's involved in this new religious sect, and they're into polygamy and—"

"He wanted you to be wife number one!" Brick didn't even try to contain his mirth. "Sounds as if he was one helluva three-star guy."

"Very funny. And you wonder why I didn't want to tell you."

That sobered him up quickly. He inhaled a deep breath and deepened his voice in an effort to wipe away every vestige of amusement. "You said no."

"Of course," she said indignantly.

"What about number two?" They were nearing the city limits so Brick eased off the gas pedal a little bit.

"He's someone I know through my catering business. I guess you'd say he's a—uh—an entertainer type. One night I finished one of my jobs and I was feeling a little down. He took me out to a bar and—"

"Wait a minute." Brick frowned and glanced at her. "What were you feeling down about?"

Lisa pushed a stray lock of hair behind her ears. "I don't know. It was temporary and he—"

"So why didn't you call me?" He pulled the car to a stop at the traffic light.

Lisa had a blank expression on her face. "I never thought of it." She shrugged. "I never had before."

Brick felt a sharp slice of pain as if she'd stabbed him and twisted the knife. It took him a moment to catch his breath. Had he really been so insensitive to her?

Lisa briefly touched his arm. "The light changed."

Brick resisted the urge to cover her hand with his. He shook his head to clear it. "Yeah." He mashed down on the accelerator. "Finish your story."

Lisa gave him a wary glance. "Well, he's from a different country, and he needs to get a green card, so he thought . . ."

Brick felt a burning sensation begin in his stomach. He patted his pocket in search of his antacid. "You said no."

"Right. I said no." Feeling extremely uncomfortable, Lisa knitted her fingers together. After this conversation, Brick was probably going to think the only kind of men she attracted were weirdos. Focusing her gaze on the road in front of them, she braced herself for a string of "I told you sos." When Brick remained silent instead, the hollow feeling inside her seemed to intensify.

Lisa slid a glance over to Brick. He appeared lost in thought. She looked at her hands again and restlessly tapped her watch. Catching sight of the time, she recalled her promise to check in with Senada. "Do you mind going by the new Renaissance Hotel? I need to see if Senada's doing all right with a party."

Brick nodded and flicked on his turn signal. "No problem."

Fifteen minutes later, Lisa and Brick were on the elevator rising to the fourth floor of Chattanooga's brand-new luxury hotel. Between the second and third floors, the car paused and jerked, and for a moment Lisa feared it was stuck. A grinding sound followed, though, and the car began moving again.

Lisa gave a nervous laugh of relief. "This elevator sounds like it needs a little work."

Brick narrowed his eyes. "Since it's a new building, they may not have gotten all the kinks out yet. I'll mention it to the manager on our way out."

The doors whooshed open. "You really didn't have to come with me. This will take only a minute."

Brick followed her down the hall. "I've never seen you in action at work."

"Since Senada's covering this party, I won't really be in on the action. I just thought I should check." She led the way to a small kitchen where a group of food servers milled around. She pulled one aside and asked for Senada, whom she learned was in the main room.

"You can wait in here if you want," she said to Brick, and slipped through a door. "I'll be right back."

Brick watched the hustle and bustle of the servers as they returned empty dessert plates to the kitchen. From bits of their conversations, he gathered that this was a pre-wedding party for a bride-to-be, and the planned entertainment was the kind that engendered sly looks and snickers.

When he heard the first strains of a tune by Prince, Brick gave into his curiosity and went into the main room. He scanned the room for Lisa, but the lights were turned down with the exception of a spotlight focused on a gyrating man.

He felt a mild amusement for the dancer until

the guy whipped off his tuxedo jacket. His shirt followed next, then Brick shook his head as the man stripped off his pants to the chorus of yells and shouts from the mostly female audience.

Brick had seen a female stripper before. He'd even had a fantasy or two about Lisa baring her body and dancing privately for him. The dance wouldn't have lasted long, though, because he wouldn't have been able to keep his hands off of her. The thought made him tug at his collar.

He'd never watched a man strut around in a G-string, sidling up to the women and thrusting his hips first this way and that.

He felt embarrassed. It was silly. Brick didn't even know the guy, but he felt embarrassed for him. Brick switched his attention to the faces of the women. They seemed transfixed by the sight of the man, eager to touch him and slip money into his G-string. Brick wondered if this was some kind of secret fantasy women had. For all his wild imagination, Brick had never considered prancing around in a bump and grind for a woman's pleasure. He pictured performing the same kind of sensual dance for Lisa and strangely enough, the notion held some appeal.

Suddenly the stripper moved across the room and tugged a woman into his arms. He whirled her in a quick suggestive tango where his hips slid against hers. Despite his discomfort, Brick felt mildly aroused. The seductive tangle of male against female reminded him of how long he'd been without Lisa.

Folding his arms over his chest, he narrowed his eyes and took a closer look at the woman who seemed to be trying to push the amorous dancer away. Brick blinked, and his discomfort, mild amusement, and arousal all burned to cinders. Fury rushed through him.

That slimy sonovabitch was dancing with Lisa.

At the front of the room, Lisa tugged one hand away only to have Henri clasp the other. "*Let me go,*" Lisa said as she pushed against his shiny, hairless chest. "You're supposed to be doing this with the guests, not me."

"But *cherie*, you inspire me. You will inspire the crowd too."

"I don't want to inspire you," she managed through gritted teeth as she freed one of her hands and backed slightly away.

"You're angry," he said, wearing a hurt expression.

Lisa felt the first tendrils of guilt wrapping around her. Henri was like an overenthusiastic puppy who was prone to mistakes. She hated hurting his feelings. Looking away, she squinted her eyes against the spotlight. "Not really," she hedged. "Go dance with the bride-to-be and I'll be much happier."

Henri nodded. "Your happiness is my greatest reward." He made one last sinuous move against her and whispered in her ear. "We must talk again of marriage."

"I don't think so," Lisa muttered, as she finally escaped Henri's clutches. She hurried over to Senada. "I can only pray that Brick missed this little spectacle."

Senada shrugged and waved for a server to bring more champagne to one of the tables. "What do you care? You said you're through with him."

"Well I am, but—" Lisa's voice dissolved into a little moan as her gaze fell on a familiar masculine form in the back of the room. Her stomach twisted into a square knot. She felt a wave of defeat. Ever since she'd begun her quest for a husband, it had seemed as if the forces of the universe were conspiring against her.

"What is it?"

Lisa took a deep breath. "You've heard the expression that God always answers prayers. Sometimes the answer is yes. Sometimes the answer is no." She started walking toward Brick. "I just got a no."

It took only a moment to reach the back of the room.

"Are you ready to go?" he asked in a low voice.

"Yes," she replied, noting that he was chewing something. It was probably one of those antacids.

Her stomach was churning so much that she was tempted to ask if she could have one too. When she saw the taut, displeased look on his face, however, she changed her mind. She'd never seen him this way before. His dark mood was so intense, Lisa could practically see it hanging around him like a heavy curtain. There was something inherently primitive and masculine in his attitude. If she'd thought it was motivated by possessiveness, Lisa would have been secretly flattered. She suspected, though, that Brick disapproved of her actions, her goals, her needs. Her. And it hurt. Lisa told herself not to care.

The brief trip to the elevator was conducted in complete silence. Brick pushed the button for the ground floor.

The interior of the elevator was gorgeous, with polished wood and mirrors all around. It provided her with a multifaceted opportunity to view Brick's impressive body and expression of disapproval no matter where she looked. Extremely uncomfortable, she stared up at the numbers and heard the distinct cracking of his knuckles. She squeezed her eyes together for a second, then opened them. She couldn't bear the silence anymore. "This is crazy. You—"

The elevator ground to a stop. She quickly looked at the numbers again. Both 2 and 3 were lit up.

Brick swore and pushed the button. He tried all of them, but nothing happened. Giving a heavy sigh, he finally looked at Lisa, his face the picture of frustration. "We're stuck."

Five minutes later, after they'd flicked the switch for the alarm and felt reasonably sure that someone was trying to fix the elevator, Lisa sank to the floor, covering her eyes with her hands. "I can't believe this night. First Henri, now this."

"Henri was the nearly naked guy who attached himself to you like a leech."

Lisa's heart sank to her feet. *Oh, no. Here it comes.* "I'm not sure I'd call him a leech," she managed. "He's from another country, and he hasn't really adapted to the American view on—on—public displays of affection."

There was a long pause. "Is Henri the green-card guy?"

Lisa heard the disbelief in his voice and kept her hands firmly over her heated face. She peeked out from between her fingers. "Yes," she whispered.

"You went out with a stripper?"

"He was dressed at the time."

"Thank God for small favors." Brick looked up at the ceiling in search of help. He shook his head. "Listen, Lisa, I know you're serious about finding a husband, but this desperation—"

The *D* word galvanized her into action. She ripped her hands away from her face and sprang to her feet. "I am not desperate! That's part of the reason I'm going through this now, so I won't be desperate when I'm getting closer to forty."

Brick saw the furious glitter in her eyes and backed off. "Okay, you're not desperate, but I'm worried about you. So far, you've gotten involved with a polygamist and a stripper."

"I wouldn't call one date getting involved."

He felt his own anger return in a rush. "Darlin'," during the first full month that we dated," he began in a low, deliberate voice, "I didn't get as close to you as that human version of Pepe Le Pew did during a single chorus of Prince's 'Cream.'"

She lifted her chin in challenge. "Well, you certainly made up for it during the last six months, wouldn't you say?"

He noted the rise and fall of her breasts through her cotton blouse and remembered what she felt like in his hands, in his mouth, pressed intimately against him. At that moment he wanted nothing more than to make love to her until they were both delirious from it. This time he would pay better attention to her needs. Although he knew what she liked, he craved the knowledge of what would drive her to the edge of pleasure. He wanted to know her inside and out. But he couldn't, and his frustration rose with the same force as his ardor. "That six months was only the beginning. There was plenty more I wanted to do with you. We may have been finished in your book, but we were far from it in mine."

He saw a quick, heady shot of desire darken her eyes and watched her nipples bead before Lisa swung away from him. "This discussion is ridiculous," she said in an unsteady voice.

Through the reflection of the mirror, he saw her wrap her arms around her chest, as if she were instinctively easing the ache of arousal. Brick might have sympathized with her if he wasn't dealing with his own throbbing need. Just to hold her would be heaven. He was perilously close to saying to hell with this friendship thing.

She shifted, and Brick heard something between a gasp and a muffled snicker.

"Pepe Le Pew?"

The deep dissatisfaction inside him eased a little at the humor he heard in her voice. He let out a long breath of air. "You gotta admit. It fits, skunk and all."

"Brick," she chided sternly. But the effect was lost when she giggled. She held up a hand. "Don't say it. I'll never be able to look at that poor man again without laughing. Think of what that will do to his ego."

He leaned against the elevator wall. "I imagine his ego can handle it," he said dryly. "But seeing the way all those women reacted to him did raise a few questions in my mind."

"Such as . . . ?"

Wondering if she was going to think he was a pervert, he paused a fraction of a moment. "Is that some kind of secret fantasy women have?"

Lisa blinked. "Fantasy?"

Brick watched her carefully. "Having a man strip and dance naked in front of you."

"You mean like Henri?"

His gaze was locked onto hers. "Henri . . . or a man who was important to you."

Lisa felt an illicit heat flow through her veins. "A man who was physically and emotionally important?"

"Yeah."

"Would this be a—uh—private performance?"

Brick nodded slowly.

Lisa sucked in a deep breath. She felt the sudden urge to fan her face. "I—uh—" She cleared her throat. "I hadn't really ever thought about it."

Brick's face was suddenly incredulous. "Really? I have. Not about a man," he said quickly. "But a woman. As a matter of fact, I fantasized about you."

Lisa decided it was time to change the subject. "Brick—"

He held up a hand. "No. Wait a minute. It was natural for me to fantasize about you when we were seeing each other. When we were apart, I thought about you all the time. And there were plenty of times that I went out of town. I had lots of fantasies about you. During that last trip, I fantasized that you stripped for me." He leaned closer to her. "I imagined you wearing one of your business suits and taking off the jacket, then slipping out of your blouse. Then you'd step out of your skirt and you'd be wearing one of those little one-piece lace things."

"A teddy," Lisa said over a very dry throat.

His eyes darkened. "Yeah, a teddy. Then I imagined reaching for you, but you would laugh and pull away. You wanted to tease, and I wanted you so much, I could barely stand it. You'd step out of these sexy high heels and undo your garters—"

"I don't wear garters," Lisa said, trying to inject a note of much-needed reality.

He gave a masculine shrug that was entirely too appealing and tossed her a killer grin. "It was *my* fantasy. When you bent to unfasten those garters," he confided, "the straps of that teddy would fall down low enough so I could see a hint of your nipples. And, Lisa, you know how much I always loved your nipples."

Lisa felt the tips of her breasts harden in response. She felt a heady, dizzying need. It made her heart pound against her rib cage, her pulse race at all her pressure points, her temples, her throat, the inside of her wrists, and between her thighs where she felt the beginning of warmth and moistness. Somewhere in her brain, however, the voice of reason rang faintly. Lisa bit her lip against a moan. Sanity, where was her sanity? "Brick," she managed, "I don't—"

"It's almost over," he coaxed in a rough tone that brought back vivid memories and sensations of when he'd been closer than close. "Babe, by that time I was begging."

FIVE

"You always seemed to want me as much as I wanted you."

Lisa closed her eyes against the tide of emotions that swept over her. His words were too intimate, but he was too far away. Her hands clenched with the need to touch him.

"The fantasy was close to real life. You kissed me and touched me and I came undone. I couldn't get enough of feeling your skin next to mine or hearing your breath hitch in your throat or watching your eyes go dark." His voice lowered. "I couldn't get enough of being inside you, Lisa. While we were together I fooled myself into believing I was the one making love to you, but now I see it was you making love to me. You—"

Lisa couldn't stand it any longer. She felt

aroused, yet torn up inside. She opened her eyes, dismayed to feel tears threaten. "No! It wasn't that way. You—"

Brick covered her lips with one finger. The honest expression in his eyes was so beautiful, it hurt. "But it was. There's too much I didn't learn about you that I still want to know."

Her heart twisted. Acutely sensitive to that slight touch of his finger against her lips, she swallowed hard. "You knew everything there was to know."

He shook his head. "I knew the mechanics. I want to know the secrets you've never told anyone. I want to know the fantasies you'll barely admit to yourself."

He asked too much. She made herself pull back. "You never seemed interested in trading secrets before," she said in a voice that quivered the way her insides did. "You always wanted things light and easy."

"Maybe things are different now."

An overwhelming sense of fear and desperation tore at her. "You said we're *friends* now."

"And we always will be," he said as if making a solemn vow.

She'd told him what she wanted! She'd laid her cards face up on the table for him to see, and he'd walked away. Lisa couldn't say it again. It hurt too much. She felt battered and bruised and didn't want her hopes raised again. If she had any sense, she'd turn away from him, but the fact of the matter was that Brick had never been so intent with her before. It was almost as if he wanted to give her everything she wanted, but something inside him prevented it. If Lisa were a fool, she'd guess that he was fighting himself far more than he was fighting her. If Lisa were a fool, she'd guess that he needed her.

"Tell me, Lisa."

She felt her heart shift as if she'd slammed into a tailspin on ice. Her head said, *get a grip*, while her emotions played tag from one end of the spectrum to the other.

The elevator jerked. Lisa glanced at the numbers at the top of the car. It was fixed, she concluded. They would be able to get out in a moment. She would be able to escape Brick's compelling, needful gaze. She would be able to escape her own conflicting feelings.

For the moment, however, her eyes were drawn back to him. The atmosphere between them was charged with intimacy, and she felt, for no logical reason, like a cheater. He'd revealed something of himself to her, and she hadn't followed suit.

She hadn't agreed to tell him anything, she told herself, but it still didn't sit well.

Lisa couldn't tell her deepest longings, of wanting a man who would love her to distraction, of wanting a man who would give her babies and forever. Her heart jerked at the mere thought.

Damn you, Brick. She sucked in a deep breath and stared straight into his violet eyes. "You want to know one of my secret fantasies?" she whispered harshly. "I've always wanted to do it in an elevator."

Instantly, his gaze darkened and he reached for her. At his first touch a spasm of wanting shook her to her soul, and she realized she could have done something very foolish if the timing had been different.

The elevator doors slid open.

Lisa jerked her gaze from Brick's, swallowed hard, and thanked her lucky stars that fate and the maintenance men had saved her from making a fool of herself again.

The following Friday night, Brick found himself staring at a choice cut of prime rib and thinking about elevators instead of enjoying his meal.

"Oh, Brick, come out, come out wherever you are," Carly said in a singsong voice.

Brick jerked his head up and saw Jarod, Troy, Carly, and Russ looking at him expectantly. They'd driven up to join him for dinner. He suspected they'd also come because they were concerned about him. Brick knew he hadn't been himself lately. He cleared his throat. "Sorry."

Carly sighed. "Is it Lisa again?" she asked in a low voice.

He lifted his drink and took a deep swallow. Although he usually detested the idea of exposing his feelings, at the moment he was too tired to give a royal rip. If his brothers bugged him too much, he was liable to forget his daddy's training and tear into them. "She's out on a blind date tonight." He took another swallow and grimaced. "Someone her wild business partner Senada found. Someone they call Mr. Perfect."

Brick wanted to chew glass.

Troy lifted a skeptical eyebrow. "You two looked as if you were getting along fine at the fair last week."

"That was last week. I haven't seen her since. She's been *busy*." God, that hurt.

Jarod frowned. "Seemed like you two were going at it pretty hot and heavy there for a while."

Brick set his beer down. "We were."

"Why did things cool off?"

Brick sucked in a deep breath of air. His privacy was extremely important to him. It was one of the reasons he'd moved away from Beulah County. But Lisa's decision to keep him at arm's length had become a thorn in his side, and he'd gotten to the point where he didn't know what he was fighting for or against anymore.

"She wanted to get married," he admitted. "I wasn't ready."

Troy shrugged. "Sounds like a no go to me. You don't want to get saddled with a pushy woman."

Carly scowled. "Troy! Lisa didn't seem pushy to me. Maybe she's simply a woman who knows what she wants. What's wrong with that?"

Russ laid a hand on Carly's clenched one. "Nothing, but most men don't like ultimatums."

"Yes, and a lot of men besides you want a committed woman at the same time that they want their freedom."

Brick shook his head. "It wasn't that way. I didn't go out with anyone else once I started seeing Lisa."

Jarod leaned forward. "Then why not marry her?"

Brick's stomach turned over, and he pushed his plate away. "I don't want to get married."

"Ever?" Troy asked. "I don't want to get hitched for the next ten or fifteen years, but I guess I might settle down by the time I'm forty."

"If you can find someone who'll have you," Carly muttered.

Troy glared at his sister. "Well, I've got fifteen years to do just that."

Impatient with the flippant exchange between Carly and Troy, Brick looked at Jarod. Although

Jarod was younger than Brick, he respected him. Jarod was the quiet, deep thinker who was currently involved in an illicit affair with the recently divorced daughter of a Beulah County doctor. The affair was at odds with the steady personality of his brother. "What about you?"

Jarod gave an ironic grin. "I'm not sure I'll ever find someone who wants me."

Carly rolled her eyes. "Give me a break. What about Clarice Douglass or Amy Burkmeir or—"

"Someone who wants me—who I want too," Jarod clarified. "But I don't think that's what Brick is talking about, is it?"

Brick rolled his shoulders restlessly. "I don't know. Don't you ever get a sick feeling in your gut at the thought of marriage? What about you, Russ? Did you ever worry that you'd get trapped in something you hated?"

Russ thought for a moment and shook his head. "I wasn't afraid of marrying Carly. I think I was more afraid of being in love with her and depending on her."

"Same thing," Brick said.

Russ shook his head again. "No. For me the commitment wasn't the issue. I wanted her committed to me if I had to hog-tie her to do it." He grinned wickedly. "At one point I did threaten to tie her up, but—"

"Russ Bradford!" Carly's face flamed. "Honestly, do you think you could keep our private life out of one discussion?"

Russ wrapped his arm around her shoulders. "Sorry, honey," he murmured in a voice that said he wasn't.

Troy shifted in his seat. "Jeez, could you guys cool it?"

"Gamophobia," Jarod said suddenly.

Brick stared at his brother again. "Gamowhat?"

"I read about it in a magazine in the dentist's office. Gamophobia is a fear of marriage or commitment. The symptoms include shortness of breath, nausea, and an unexplained panic at the mere mention of marriage." He lifted his hands. "I'm no shrink, but you might want to look into it."

Brick felt his whole world dip and sway. "Gamophobia?" he repeated in disbelief. It couldn't be, he thought. A phobia? Not him. Absolutely, positively not him. "What else did it say?"

"That men suffered from this particular phobia more often than women and that it's treated with some of the same techniques people use to get over claustrophobia, fear of flying, and other phobias. It said something about how it correlates with other intimacy issues, but I didn't get to read the whole article."

Brick's stomach rolled again. "Treated," he said in distaste.

"Yeah," Jarod said thoughtfully, lifting his beer to his mouth. "By a psychologist."

Brick spent the rest of the evening trying to grasp the idea of gamophobia. The whole thing sounded like a bunch of crap designed by psychologists to get more money out of people. Sure, he'd had a few little fears, but he'd always dealt with them or found a way around them. On the occasions he'd used explosives to accomplish a demolition job, his attitude had been one of respect rather than fear. There was no place for nerves when a man was blasting a rock foundation in a matter of seconds. That situation, like most of his jobs, called for planning, preparation, and expertise.

If pressed, Brick would have to say he got a rush when a challenging job was completed.

If pressed to discuss his feelings about marriage, however, Brick would have to say he broke into a cold sweat. Which left him with an uneasy suspicion.

On Saturday afternoon after he checked one of his job sites, he drove to the local library to prove to himself that gamophobia didn't apply to him.

Three hours later, he left the library more troubled than ever. The summer heat was stifling inside his Thunderbird even with the T-top down. He started the ignition, flicked the air conditioner on max, and sat there.

He missed her.

It was far more than physical, he was learning, and he was surprised he hadn't realized it before. He missed the way they'd sat together and watched a sports game. She was always getting her terms mixed up, he remembered with faint humor. She couldn't tell a run from a field goal, and she'd been known to make him miss a great play because she had asked him to explain something at a crucial moment. The night before he'd watched a Braves game, and it hadn't been nearly as much fun without Lisa.

She'd taken the joy, he realized. Joy was a hokey word, but it described what being with her meant to him.

He'd heard a kid banging out "Chopsticks" on a television commercial and remembered when she'd tried to make his broad hands hammer out that same song at a party they'd gone to last winter.

Looking at his hands, he felt that yawning ache again. He drummed his fingertips on the steering wheel and thought about the conversation he'd had with his family. One comment Carly had made about Russ stuck in Brick's mind. As they were leaving Brick had joked with Carly to let him know if Russ ever stepped out of line.

She'd laughed and said, "Not likely." Then her

expression had turned serious. "You know, he's always been there for me. Good or bad. And especially when times were tough." She'd smiled. "Guess I'm pretty lucky."

Brick thought both of them were lucky, along with Daniel and Sara, and Garth and Erin. It was strange how much he wanted to be with Lisa, yet the thought of marriage still made him feel sick. *Gamophobia.*

Brick shook his head, refusing to think about it anymore. He couldn't do a damn thing about it today, anyway. He could, however, start being there for Lisa. He was at a loss when it came to romantic gestures and writing gushy poems, but he could handle being there.

He remembered Lisa was overseeing a party. Checking his watch, he realized he had a few hours to kill, so he decided to get her a birthday present. He moved the car into gear and frowned at his reflection in the rearview mirror. Better late than never. So he hoped.

Lisa pulled into a parking space near her apartment and rested her head on the steering wheel. It had been a wretched day from beginning to end. Her body ached from head to toe. Tired to the point of being dizzy, she considered curling up in the seat and spending the night right there.

A gentle thump-thump sounded on her window. She jerked upright and saw Brick. For a moment, she wondered if she was imagining things.

"Are you okay?"

Even through the closed window, she heard the concern in his voice. Her heart clutched. *No.* Lisa turned her head in an indecisive circle, but lowered her window, and flipped the automatic locks. She took a calming breath. "C'mon in. I'm trying to get my fourth wind, so I can crawl to my door and collapse in bed."

Instead of joining her in the car, he crouched down beside her window. "Sounds as if you had a rough day."

This time Lisa nodded emphatically.

"You look tired." He rose and opened her door, flipped the locks again, and rolled up her window. "Wanna ride to your apartment?"

Confused, Lisa looked at the curb directly in front of her car. "I think I'm already here."

Brick gave a slow grin and shook his head. "I'll carry you."

Lisa's eyes rounded as she grabbed her purse and slid one foot out of her car. "No, no, no, no. I'm too tall, too heavy, too—"

"Not for me." Pulling her up into his arms, he nudged the car door shut with one knee and walked toward her front door.

Totally flustered, Lisa pushed at his chest while her purse dangled beneath her. It was unsettling enough that she was being carried, but the other feelings that assaulted her because she was in Brick's arms again overwhelmed her. "You really didn't have to—"

"Where's your key?" he asked, ignoring her protests.

He'd probably forgotten that she weighed a ton, she thought glumly. "You can put me down now." Lisa jiggled her keys from the side pocket of her purse. "You can put—"

"Inside," he told her, waiting while she fumbled with the key.

He pushed the door open, turned on the hall light, and walked toward the living room. When he still didn't put her down, she became acutely aware of his heart pounding against her hand. "Brick," she said in a strained voice, "please put me—"

He set her down on the sofa. "There. I didn't break a sweat and I'm not breathing heavy," he mocked.

"Don't blame me if you get a hernia," she muttered, still feeling self-conscious.

"You worry too much."

"In case you haven't noticed, I'm not a small woman."

His gaze instantly trapped hers. "I noticed." His voice lowered intimately. "But maybe you've forgotten how much I noticed."

Lisa got a strong indication that he wouldn't

mind showing her all over again. Her skin suddenly felt flushed with heat.

"It's no difficulty having you in my arms, Lisa. In case you haven't noticed, I'm not a small man," he arrogantly echoed her earlier statement. "Anytime you need someone to carry you, let me know."

As if she could forget anything about his body! The image was branded on her brain. Lisa put a clamp on her imagination. "I hope I won't be needing anyone to carry me anywhere."

He shrugged. "If you *want* to be carried, I'm capable of that too." He grinned slyly. "You think I deserve a star for that?"

She should give him a star for driving her crazy. Lisa gave him a dark look.

"Don't answer that. What do you want to drink?"

She sat up, abruptly aware that she was letting a guest serve her in her own house. Her upbringing wouldn't allow it. He'd flustered her so much, she'd forgotten her manners. "Oh, no. I can get it. I—"

Brick's hands fastened on her shoulders, holding her in place. His violet gaze was intent, yet gentle. "You're tired, remember? I'm getting you something to drink," he said firmly. "What do you want?"

"I don't want to be rude."

"You're not."

"My mother would have my head."

Brick leaned closer and whispered, "I promise I won't tell her."

Lisa's lips twitched at the conspiratorial expression on his face. Caught between wanting to argue and give in, she surrendered, sinking back on the pillows and covering her face with one hand. "Okay. You win. Thank you for carrying me. And I'd love some lemonade?"

He squeezed her shoulders, then stood. "Sit tight."

Kicking off her shoes, she watched him go out the front door and wondered why he'd gone back outside. She was also starting to wonder why he'd shown up at all when he quickly returned with a small wrapped box.

"Just a minute," he called as he went into the kitchen.

A moment later he entered the living room with the lemonade and the box. He presented her with both and flicked on a small table lamp. Lifting her feet, he sat at the other end of the sofa. "Happy Birthday, Lisa."

Lisa's heart contracted. She stared at the gaily wrapped present. "But—"

"I know it's late, but if I'd had any idea your birthday was coming, I would have wanted to be a part of it. I still do."

Lisa set the lemonade on a coaster, and her gaze flew to Brick's. "I don't know what to say."

He shrugged. "Why don't you open it?"

With a strange sense of nervousness, she tugged the ribbon and paper loose, then lifted the top off the box. Nestled inside were exquisitely crafted cut-crystal figures of a mother deer and her fawn.

Lisa held her breath for a long moment. There was a significance to the gift. Brick had always told her she reminded him of a doe because of her big eyes and sometimes shy nature. She didn't like for strangers to use pet names with her, but when Brick did, it somehow felt different. The figures were beautiful, reminding her afresh of her desire for her own baby. She could speculate that the nature of the gift meant that Brick had at least accepted her desire to have a child even if he couldn't be a part of it.

That thought tore at her. Too many poignant emotions pulled her in different directions. She felt an overwhelming urge to cry. Clearing her throat, she carefully set the figurines on the sofa table. "They're beautiful, Brick. Just beautiful."

"You like them?" His large hand wrapped around one of her stocking-clad feet.

"Absolutely. I'll treasure them. Thank you." Her gaze met his, and she had the odd sensation of sharing some rapport with a trapped doe.

His thumb moving across the ball of her foot, he simply looked at her without saying a word. But his eyes, oh, his eyes were full of things that stirred her soul and made her heart pound. Full of things she simply couldn't believe.

Lisa cleared her throat. "What—what are you doing?"

"Rubbing your feet. Didn't you say you were tired?"

Lisa blinked. "Well, yes, but—"

"Doesn't that include your feet?"

He continued the gentle massage along her inner arch, and she nearly groaned. "Yes, but I don't know. I . . ." She sighed when he squeezed her heel.

"Tell me about your day," he invited in an easy voice.

Despite her reserve, Lisa felt herself respond to his relaxed tone. She should probably tell him to get his wonderful hands off her feet, his great body off her sofa, and leave her alone. He rubbed the back of her ankle, and she bit back a whimper as her tensed muscles began to ease. The spirit was willing, but the flesh was weak, Lisa told herself and immediately knew the old adage didn't apply.

Who was she kidding? She was one spineless puddle of femininity in dire need of a little TLC. If Brick was willing to rub her feet and offer some consolation, who was she to reject the offer?

It wasn't as if he was doing anything the least bit provocative, she thought. His hands had a long way to go before he reached her knees, let alone her thighs, or hips, or . . . Blocking off that thought, Lisa concentrated on the soothing effect of his hands and let out a long sigh.

"It all started when I backed over Mrs. Crabapple's groceries. Six bags. Eggs, meat, canned goods, and ten glass jars of prune juice."

"Mrs. Crabapple?" he echoed, amusement filtering through his voice.

"My neighbor. She can be nice, but she has a little problem with irregularity, so she was really upset about losing her prune juice." Lisa heard a muffled snicker and sank deeper into the sofa. "Go ahead and laugh. It gets worse. I cleaned up the mess and agreed to go get her some prune juice." She paused and arched her foot into his hand.

"And?" he prompted.

"And one of my tires was flat."

"Oh, Lisa." He chuckled and shook his head. "Who changed it for you?"

The sympathy in his tone warmed her enough to bring a wry grin to her lips. "You mean after I tried to change it myself?"

Brick looked at her in astonishment.

"Yes. The manager of my apartment complex wasn't amused. He said I was blocking traffic and generally being a nuisance. The whole time he was changing my tire, he was cursing women drivers."

"Did you beat him up?"

Lisa laughed. "No. I was running late."

"Want me to get him?" he said with a half serious growl.

Lisa tossed him a grateful look. "That's okay. Knowing me, I'll probably mow down his groceries sometime."

"You're being too hard on yourself."

"No, I'm not," she said truthfully. "But you're very generous to say so."

He switched his attention to her other foot and began the same mesmerizing treatment.

"Ooooh," Lisa said, closing her eyes. "You've got incredible hands."

Brick saw the expression of bliss on her face and remembered another time when she'd looked that way and had said those very same words. He'd been inside her.

He took a deep breath and worked his fingers around her little toe. The atmosphere felt suddenly, ridiculously intimate. The skirt of her dress had ridden up to the bottom of her thighs. If things had been different between them, he would skim his hands up her calves, past her knees to her thighs. He'd push her skirt up and pull her stockings down so that he could touch her silky legs. And when he was finished caressing her legs, he would slip his fingers inside her panties where she was wet and warm and soft.

And if he continued that line of thought, he

would go crazy. Brick tightened his jaw at the same time that he gently squeezed Lisa's shapely foot.

She moaned, and the soft sound was so sensual that he grimaced. His forehead beaded with perspiration. She squirmed, and the little movement made her skirt ride up a little higher.

Brick chewed on the inside of his cheek. He needed to distract himself. "How was the job tonight?" he forced himself to ask.

"Twenty extra guests showed up and three servers didn't show up. It took everything I had to stretch the food, and I think I ran at least ten miles in dress shoes, but . . ." she paused and smiled triumphantly. "I did it, and they booked their awards banquet with me." Her eyelids drooped. She was growing drowsy. "This is so nice of you, Brick. Ooooh, so nice. An angel must have sent you over here tonight."

Brick wasn't feeling the least bit angelic. He was itching to expand the territory his hands were massaging. Every breath she took dug its way a little deeper into his gut, a little deeper into his blood. He narrowed his eyes and ruthlessly raised the subject most likely to put out the fire in his blood.

"You haven't mentioned your date last night," he managed in a gruff tone. "Was Mr. Perfect as perfect as you've been told?"

Lisa opened her eyes. "He was—nice. Actually,

he was more than nice. Intelligent and tall with a good sense of humor."

Brick felt his stomach twist at her words. He hated this guy already.

"I liked him."

His chest constricted. "Is that so?" he murmured, telling himself that like was a long way from love.

"I'm going out with him again next weekend." Her eyes drooped again, and she covered a yawn with her hand. "He kinda reminds me of you."

Brick felt the ground shift beneath him. "Oh, really?"

"Uh-huh. Except he doesn't have your aversion to marriage."

SIX

Brick barely restrained the urge to roar.

Mr. Perfect reminded Lisa of him!

Brick knew his blood pressure was climbing into the red-flag range. His response to her little comment was all out of proportion, but he couldn't seem to help it. Brick remembered how at the beginning of their relationship he had used every opportunity to advance the sexual intimacy between them. If Mr. Perfect was just like Brick, he would be thinking the same way, making the same moves.

The possibilities of what could develop between Lisa and this guy went off in his mind like charges detonating at millisecond intervals.

The guy would kiss her. He would hold her.

For God's sake, the guy would make love to

her. Worse yet, the guy might take Brick's place in Lisa's life and end up marrying her.

Brick couldn't remain still one second longer. Energy pulsed through his veins, compelling him to move. He wanted to yell. He wanted to run. He wanted to beat the crap out of Mr. Perfect. He sucked in a deep breath of air and stared at Lisa. He was ready to lose it, and *she was sleeping*. He carefully shifted her feet off his lap and eased up from the sofa.

Lacing his fingers together, he cracked his knuckles. The action didn't begin to quell his agitation. He still wanted to ram his hand through a wall. He rubbed his hands over his face, then scooped up the lemonade and took it into the kitchen. Eyeing the glass, he snitched a sip in hopes that it would cool him off.

But he still felt as if his skin were pulled too tight for his body. He went back in the living room and decided he couldn't leave her sleeping on the couch, so he lifted her in his arms and carried her to her bed. It had been a long time since he'd been in her bedroom, and the awful realization hit him that another man could be taking his place in her bed soon.

He ground his teeth. Outrage suffused him from head to toe. "The William Tell Overture" played in his mind, and as he settled Lisa on the bed, her eyelids fluttered.

Abruptly realizing that he'd begun to whistle, he bit his tongue. She gave a soft sigh, turned onto her side, and fell back to sleep.

Still hearing the clanging of cymbals and the racing music, Brick backed out of her bedroom. Turning off the lights, he concentrated fiercely on making a soundless exit. He locked her front door, pulled it shut behind him, and made his way to his car. As soon as he shut his car door and started the engine, he began to whistle again.

His eyes weren't violet, Lisa thought, but they lit with humor and masculine appreciation. He was tall, but not quite as tall as Brick. And his voice was different, more of a tenor than a baritone.

He had a great smile, and he was currently smiling at her.

Lisa concentrated, waiting for that pleasurable little flip her stomach would take at receiving the undivided attention of such an attractive man.

She waited while sterling silver met china and fine crystal reflected candlelight throughout the restaurant. She waited, and nothing happened.

"Is your filet mignon okay?" Greg Dawson asked in his smooth voice.

"Fine," she said quickly, wondering why her stomach hadn't flipped. "It's great." She mustered a smile. "You mentioned you were in construction. What kind of things do you do?"

"Right now I'm working in conjunction with a demolition expert on a factory. He's tearing out part of it while I'm working on an addition."

Her attention snagged on the mention of the demolition expert. She took a sip of her wine. "Sounds as if it could get complicated."

"It can," he conceded. "Equipment availability is one of the biggest problems, but I'll tell you, if you're working with someone decent, it can make all the difference in the world. This time I'm working with Brick—"

"Brick?" Lisa repeated, gripping her glass. "Brick, as in Pendleton?"

"Yeah. You've met him?"

She nodded. "He's a—a—friend."

"Small world, isn't it? He's reasonable, doesn't have a short fuse. Great to work with." He took a bite of his T-bone steak and chewed thoughtfully. "How'd you meet him?"

Lisa searched for an easy explanation. "I met him at the Watering Hole. You know how crowded it is on Friday nights," she rushed on, trying to cover her discomfort. "Sometimes I think everyone in Chattanooga has shown up there at one time or another."

"Probably," Greg agreed. "And you say you're friends." He chuckled.

Confused by his amusement, Lisa nodded hesitantly. "Why do—"

"Must have been an off night." Greg shook his head and swept her with a warm, flirty gaze. "I'm surprised he didn't take one look at you and try to elope."

Lisa felt her cheeks heat. Brick certainly hadn't said anything about eloping on their first meeting, but his eyes had said far more than "How do you do? Pleased to meet you." She felt a quick surprising stab of pain. If only things could have been different. Stupid, she scolded herself. *Stop feeling sorry for yourself.* After all, Greg was not only the most promising date she'd had since she'd started her mate hunt, he was nice, tall, and attractive. Great genes, she mentally added to his long list of attributes, and he'd probably be a great father.

She brought her attention back to the conversation at hand. "I'm sure eloping was the last thing on his mind," Lisa assured him.

Greg raised an eyebrow and lowered his voice. "His loss." He lifted his glass to hers in a salute.

His loss. So it was. Lisa met Greg's gaze and nodded, then drank the wine. At that moment, Lisa became determined to keep her mind off Brick and on Greg for the rest of the evening.

She let him coax her into dancing with him for a few numbers, and refused to remember the time she and Brick had danced in her apartment. She laughed at his jokes, let him hold her hand, and tried not to think about how Brick's hands had felt as he'd massaged her feet the other night.

By the time they arrived at her door, however, Lisa was starting to feel the beginning of desperation. She was out with a wonderful man, a man who was obviously attracted to her, and she was expending more energy trying *not* to think about Brick than she was trying to attract Greg.

For crying out loud, what was wrong with her?

A kiss. Kisses were magic, she thought. Kisses could wipe away tears, sadness, and memories. Under the gentle glow of her porch light, she decided then and there that she would kiss Greg Dawson and she absolutely positively would not think of Brick.

"I had a good time tonight." He tugged her a little closer.

"Thank you for inviting me. I did too."

"Can I call you again?"

"Sure." His eyes were very brown, she thought. A nice brown, but brown wasn't violet. She mentally swore.

He lowered his head until his lips were close to hers. "I guess it's time to say good night."

"Guess so," Lisa echoed, waiting for the rush of pleasure she was praying for. Perhaps if she shut her eyes, she thought, and immediately closed them. She held her breath in anticipation.

Finally his mouth touched hers. It was a gentle rubbing of his lips against hers. With a different man, the movement would have been unbearably sensual.

It didn't do a thing for her.

Damn. She stood there hoping for that little flip in her belly. She waited for her heart to speed up.

Frustration edged through her. Maybe if she took a more active role, the sparks would start to fly. She puckered her lips, and he seemed to get the message, deepening the kiss.

After a moment, he gradually pulled away, his eyes turbulent with passion and displeasure. "Who is it?"

Lisa's heart clutched. "Who is what?"

Greg shook his head. "You kissed me like a woman who's trying to forget another man and having a tough time doing it. Pretending insults both of us, Lisa," he admonished.

Feeling embarrassed and defeated, she let out a heavy sigh. "I'm sorry. You don't know how sorry," she nearly wailed. "If you weren't so nice, I could hate you for being so perceptive."

"How long has it been?"

Lisa shrugged. She was totally disgusted with herself. "Obviously not long enough." She pulled her keys from her bag in a rough movement. "I can't tell you how sorry I am."

"Me too," he said, a hint of humor coming back into his voice.

She glanced up at him and thought, *Lord, why can't I fall for him?* "The woman who gets you is going to be very lucky," she said sincerely.

He gave a half grin. "I know."

Lisa laughed. "This is horrible, and you're making me laugh."

He shook his head. "It could be worse." He pulled a card from his pocket and pressed it into her hand. "Tell you what, when you get over whatsisname, give me a call."

Lisa nodded and wished him good night. But when she got inside her apartment, she wasn't wondering when she'd get over Brick. She wondered *if* she'd get over Brick.

Lisa rose at the insane hour of four-thirty A.M. on Monday morning. Still disgusted with her lack of lust toward Greg Dawson, she muttered to herself as she pulled on her jeans and a T-shirt. She had no business going anywhere with Brick, let alone to a scheduled blasting for the office expansion that morning, but she'd agreed to this last week before the disaster with Greg had occurred. She'd tried calling Brick to cancel, but his answering machine wasn't working.

She yanked a hairbrush through her hair and

clipped it at her nape. It wasn't a date, Brick had assured her. His company's central office had called and asked him to do the blasting since the regular blaster wasn't available. Brick had recalled that Lisa had said she would love to watch him do "a shot" sometime. It had all seemed innocent, yet interesting.

Now Lisa wasn't so sure.

Her doorbell rang, and she scowled into the mirror. Not one speck of makeup adorned her face. She couldn't be accused of trying to slay Brick with her beauty, she thought, as she grabbed her tennis shoes from the closet and went to open the door.

Her stomach flipped at the sight of him. Darn. Lisa frowned. "Hi. Just let me get my shoes on and I'll be ready."

Brick's eyebrows shot up at her tone. He watched her concentrate on tying the shoelaces. She looked fresh scrubbed, but sleepy, and he found himself recalling the time they'd gone sledding this past winter. He'd coaxed her into trying it for fifteen minutes. She'd loved flying down the hill so much, they'd stayed for an hour. It was one of her characteristics that tugged at his heart. Lisa needed to be coaxed sometimes. Brick felt a gentling inside him. "I've got some coffee for you in the car."

"Thanks."

He stifled a smile and followed her out the door. "Not a morning person, huh?"

"Not if four-thirty is considered morning. How long did you do blasting for this construction company? I wouldn't have lasted a week."

"Some guys don't." He opened his car door. "I was a blaster for ten years, did a ton of traveling, and got sick to death of hotel rooms, so I told my boss I needed a change. You already know that he put me in charge of the Chattanooga branch for demolition services two years ago, and the rest is history." He took the lid off the coffee and handed it to her. "There you go."

Lisa pursed her lips and blew, then took a few quick sips. "Thanks."

She sounded more sincere this time. Her eyelids hooded with drowsiness, Lisa reminded him of a sleepy kitten, and he thought that if it were the best of circumstances, he'd kiss her awake. If it were the best of circumstances, he wouldn't feel as if he were walking through a mine field. "I wouldn't have thought you would need a shot of caffeine to get you started in the morning."

She met his gaze briefly. "You haven't been around me much in the morning, though, have you?"

Touché. The kitten had claws. He watched her slide into the seat, and he closed the door for her. He wrinkled his brow thoughtfully. Something was wrong, and it was more than morning grumpiness. He sensed her displeasure, dark and deep. His gut twisted with the ache he'd felt ever since Lisa had left him. He wanted to be the man she turned to for whatever she needed. He wanted to be the one to whom she confessed what she'd backed into with her car. He wanted her laughter, tears, victories, and failures. Dammit to hell, he wanted it all, but an endless doubt in something more obscure than wedding rings kept the devil at his heels.

Brick took a quick sip of his own coffee and tossed the rest of it. His thoughts brought enough of a bitter taste to his mouth without adding black coffee.

Reining in his dark mood, he got in the car and headed toward the site. Lisa still hadn't spoken several minutes later. "You're quiet. Is something on your mind?"

"I'm not sure my mind is working yet."

Brick relaxed slightly. "Everything okay with your family? You haven't mentioned them much lately."

"My youngest sister, Janine, is renovating an old house with her new husband. My other sisters told her that if her marriage can survive this, it'll survive anything." Lisa laughed. "I think she and her husband have already agreed not to wallpaper together."

Brick stopped at a traffic light and looked at Lisa. "I didn't know Janine had gotten married. When did that happen?"

Lisa looked away. "It was in May around my birthday. I think you might have been out of town for a few weeks then."

"Seems as if I missed a number of things when I was out of town that time." He frowned, adding the new information and wondering what to make of it. "So all three of your younger sisters are married now. Renee is married to the guy in the air force. Tina and—"

"Jeff," she supplied. "He's a plumber, and they live in Memphis a few blocks from my parents."

All married except for her. Brick wondered if that was part of the reason she'd been so hell-bent on marriage. He would be crazy to ask her about it. Crazy was about right. He took the plunge. "Do your parents ever talk to you about getting married?"

Brick felt her stiffen beside him.

"Not a lot," she said in a quiet voice. "My dad teased me a little at Janine's wedding when I didn't catch the wedding bouquet. My mother asked when I was going to let them meet you."

Brick sensed a formidable resistance in her, but he'd gotten to the place where he wanted to understand everything about Lisa. "What was your answer?"

Lisa hesitated. "I told her you were busy with work. She said something about wishing you'd come to the wedding, and I dropped it."

"Why?"

"In case you've forgotten, weddings are about commitment," she said, exasperation leaking into her tone. "The whole situation would have driven you crazy."

"Maybe," he conceded. "Maybe not. I wish you had asked. I would have liked to meet your family."

Brick felt her stare at him.

"Are you saying you would have gone?"

"I don't know," he said carefully. "I would have made the effort if I thought it was something you'd wanted. Weddings are about family too."

Lisa shook her head and folded her arms. "I don't believe you."

Brick felt a jab of temper as they neared the construction site. "But you don't know, do you? Because you never asked me."

"You wanted everything nice and easy. No strings."

"I did," he confessed, and pulled the car to a stop. When he saw that she wasn't going to look at him, he tucked his thumb under her chin and coerced her into meeting his gaze. "But tell me one time I wasn't interested in you. As a friend, as a businesswoman, as a lover. Hell, as a woman who backs her car into something new on a weekly basis. Name one time."

Her eyes were wide with trepidation. He wanted

them wide with wonder. He wanted to kiss her, to match her mouth to his and cut this silliness between them.

Guided by an innate awareness of her sensuality, he did the next best thing to a kiss and rubbed his thumb across her lips. Back and forth, back and forth, until he gently pressed his finger into her mouth. She instinctively pursed her lips around it, and his loins tightened.

He slowly removed his thumb and lifted it to his lips. "You can't name a time, because there's never been one," he whispered hoarsely. "In a minute, we're getting out of this car, and I can't think about you anymore. I can't think about how much I want to hold you. I can't think about how I'd like to kiss you for the next hour and not come up for air. I can't think about how you feel underneath that T-shirt and those jeans, and how much I've missed touching you, or I could screw up this job."

Staring into her turbulent aroused eyes, he took a deep breath and grabbed the hard hats on the dash. "Here's your hat. I'll introduce you to the super, and then I want you to watch it all. I want you to notice what the foundation looks like before and what it looks like after. And after it's all over, we'll talk."

Wrapping his hand around hers, he tugged her out of the car and toward the site. Lisa automatically followed where he led, but her head was spinning. She didn't know what to think or say. At the moment, she could only feel. Her lips still burned from his touch and her heart was beating so hard, it felt as if it were clanging in her chest. God help her, she didn't think she'd ever recover from hearing Brick say those things.

For the first time, Lisa wondered if this meant that no matter what she'd said about breaking off their relationship, Brick wasn't going anywhere. Her stomach twisted at the notion. She fought a wild elation at the same time she told herself that it didn't matter. She and Brick were miles apart when it came to the future.

Somehow she responded to the superintendent's greeting, but her mind was still on Brick. What he'd said wouldn't go away. It was the kind of declaration she'd dreamed of. The only words missing had been "I love you," and "Will you marry me?"

Lisa bit her lip as a cold, hard dose of reality hit, because she knew she wasn't likely to ever hear those crucial missing words.

Two trucks pulled into the gravel parking lot, and the drivers immediately called for Brick. An instinct for emotional survival kicked in and made her deliberately stop thinking about what Brick had said. Instead she took stock of her surroundings. At this time in the morning, there wasn't a great deal of traffic. The construction site was surrounded by a wire fence and in the darkness before dawn, to

Lisa's inexperienced eye, it looked like a lot of machinery, dirt, and rock.

The rock was the problem. Construction for the addition couldn't continue until the foundation was excavated. Watching more closely, she narrowed her eyes and saw that Brick was examining the holes drilled for the explosives.

By sunup, he was loading the holes with cartridged explosives. "Why cartridged explosives?" she asked the man beside her.

The young man pointed toward the office building. "If we overload and there's flyrock, a lot of people could get hurt. Windows could get broken."

She looked at the intricate design of holes, connectors, and wires, and shook her head at the complexity of such a small project. "How does he know where to put everything and how much to use?"

He shrugged. "It takes years of experience. Brick's the best. That's why the operating manager of the company tried to keep him blasting as long as he could."

It gave her an entirely new perspective on Brick. It seemed as if he checked the "shot" at least ten times. Back and forth, he looked for anything he could have missed. So utterly cautious, she thought, and wondered if the same cautiousness spilled over into his emotional commitment.

Was he the kind of man who would have to

walk over the same ground time and time again before he took that final step?

The notion didn't set her mind at ease, but it did give her something else to think about, something she knew would stay in the back of her mind for a long time.

Brick put wire mats over each hole, then brought the leads to the protected area where she stood.

"Go ahead and sound the warning signal," he told the man beside her.

A loud horn blast jolted Lisa. Covering her ears, she nearly jumped out of her skin.

Brick seemed oblivious to the noise, but noticed her reaction. He grinned. "How would you like to wake up to that every morning instead of your clock radio?"

She laughed in disbelief. "About as much as you would."

"I'll pass. Get ready."

She watched him connect the wires and pick up something the size of a pencil. "What is that?" she asked the young man, not wanting to distract Brick.

He must have heard anyway. "We call it a popper. It's a nonelectric detonator. It's safer than the old kind." He received clearance from the superintendent on a radio. Then Brick surveyed the site again and called out, "Fire in the hole!"

Within less than a second, the ground was rocked by the explosion and the noise was deafening. Lisa had to resist the urge to crouch down. It was silly, but she kept expecting someone to say, "Hit the deck!" The rock looked as if it had turned into a dust cloud. It was an incredible sight, watching all that hard rock instantly shattered. Even though she'd known what was going to happen, she hadn't expected to be awed by the power of the explosion.

"You better close your mouth or you'll be eating a lot of dust, Lisa," Brick said dryly.

Lisa knew the voice of experience when she heard it. She closed her mouth.

A little over an hour later, after Brick had inspected the shot and filled out paperwork, they left the site. "How about we get a fast-food lunch and take it to my apartment. I need to grab a shower."

Lisa agreed and barraged him with questions the whole way to his home. Brick patiently answered all of them and translated some of the technical jargon.

It wasn't until he took his shower that she realized it was the first time she'd been inside his apartment. She remembered wishing for this. Senada had said she was silly, but Lisa had always wanted Brick to take her to his personal space.

Now that Lisa was there, she didn't know where to look first. He probably watched his

Braves games in the lounger that occupied the prize spot in front of the television, she guessed. Her gaze skipped over the large comfortable sofa that occupied one wall to the CD system housed on a small shelving unit. Country-western and rock CDs lay on one of the shelves. Nary a classical one contaminated the bunch, she noticed with a grin. On the bottom shelf were several photo albums.

Her fingers itched to open them and learn the secrets of Brick's past. The temptation was great enough that she would have except she suspected he'd be out of the shower very soon.

With a reluctant sigh, she moved away from the albums and found a collection of photos on the wall. All family, she suspected. There were pictures of three different weddings. Carly and Russ's, Erin and Garth's, and Daniel and Sara's. The rest were assorted pictures taken with his brothers, except for one older looking photo.

"That's my mom and dad," Brick said from the hallway.

Lisa quickly turned and looked at him. His hair was still wet. He'd left his shirt unbuttoned, and she could see a smattering of droplets on his chest. For some reason, the sight made her thirsty. She swallowed. "I didn't hear the shower cut off."

He gave a slow grin. "Maybe your hearing was damaged by that blast horn."

"Maybe," she agreed, feeling his humor grab something inside her and pull. "I like your apartment."

He shrugged. "It's a place to eat and sleep, not as nice as yours."

She tilted her head to one side, considering what he'd said. "Is that why you never brought me here, when we were—" She searched for a word. Dating didn't seem to quite cover it. "When we were—"

"Together," Brick finished for her. "I always liked being at your place better than mine. Yours felt more like a home." He paused and studied her. "Did it bother you that I didn't bring you here?"

"Oh, no," Lisa said too quickly. "I assumed it was more convenient for you, or that maybe you needed your privacy."

He lifted an eyebrow in disbelief. "Why do I think I missed the boat on this one too?"

"No, really," she said in a tone rife with undercurrents of embarrassment. "I didn't think—"

Ignoring her protest, Brick hooked his fingers around her wrist and tugged. "Let me give you the nickel tour." As he led her down the hallway, the reason he'd tried to keep his relationship with her so isolated from the rest of his life hit him in the face. His time with her had been so special, he hadn't wanted to share it. Being with Lisa always made him feel as if he'd come home. Sighing, he wished he could find a way to tell her that now. He watched her carefully, wondering if it would make a difference to her.

"A seascape," Lisa said, pointing to the picture above his king-size bed in his bedroom.

"Yeah, it's the one drawback to living in Tennessee. No ocean."

"I know what you mean. I keep wishing I could get to the beach." Her eyes widened as if she'd just remembered something. "As a matter of fact, I'll be going on a weekend cruise next month."

Brick's grin froze on his face. "With Mr. Perfect?" he tried to say in a normal voice.

Lisa shook her head. "No. That dating service I told you about is sponsoring a cruise, so I signed up." Her hands fluttered until she clasped them together. "You never know," she said with a shrug as her gaze slid from his. "Moonlight, music, and island breezes might stir something up."

She sounded as if she were hoping to be stirred, and Brick wanted to be the one doing the stirring. He laced his fingers together and caught himself before he cracked his knuckles.

"Let's eat," he said, then started whistling. He used the opportunity to put his hand around her elbow and stopped at the doorway. "So what did you think of the shot?"

She turned, and her face was suddenly close to his. The area was small and the hallway was dark. He smelled the soft scent of her perfume and felt more intimate with her than he had in a long time. He looked deep into her eyes and felt the air crackle around him. She had to feel it, he thought. She had to feel this pull that never went away. "It just seems to get stronger," he murmured to himself, wanting to touch a stray strand of her hair. Instead he let his hand slide from her arm to the inside of her wrist and rubbed the place where her pulse beat swiftly.

Lisa glanced at his hand, but didn't remove hers. "It what?" she asked in a hushed voice.

He shook his head. "Nothing. I asked what you thought of the shot."

He watched her throat move in a deep swallow. "It was incredible. So powerful. It was amazing to me that those explosives and little wires had the power to turn that rock to dust." She shook her head. "Amazing."

He lifted her hand to his bare chest, where his own heart pounded like thunder. "Maybe you'll understand me a little better now."

"What do you mean?" she whispered as if whispering were the best she could manage.

Brick felt a lick of arousal wind its way to his

belly. "You saw what dynamite did to that foundation." He lowered his head and gave into the temptation to unfasten the clip in her hair. "Lisa, you do the same thing to me."

SEVEN

Lisa's heart soared into her throat. With his hands in her hair and his pulse drumming against her palm, she felt weak. She stifled a plea for help or maybe it was a plea for him. Confused, she dropped her hand away.

His broken groan caused a knot in her chest. "For God's sake, Lisa, touch me. Anywhere or everywhere, but touch me."

It was too much. She tried to look away, but his violet gaze kept her trapped more surely than an armed guard. The need in his eyes compelled her to surrender to her own bottled-up desires. Her whole body seemed to cry out to be close to him.

Tentatively, she lifted her hands to his face.

When her palms met his skin, he closed his eyes as if her touch were almost too pleasurable to bear. "Brick," she whispered hesitantly, "I don't—"

He turned his mouth into her hand and kissed it. "Just don't stop." He shuddered when she slid her hands through his still-damp hair. He coiled his own fingers through her hair. "I don't want to open my eyes. I'm afraid you'll disappear. Maybe you're another dream. Maybe you're not real."

A lump rose in her throat. Lisa swallowed hard. "I'm real, Brick. I've always been real." Driven by the overriding desire to prove it, she stepped closer so that her body pressed against his, her sensitive breasts to his hard chest, her belly to his swollen ridge. Her thighs parted for his leg to fit between them. Stretching on tiptoe, she gave into another desire and matched her lips to his.

Her lips were wet, warm satin, and her sweet taste made Brick ravenous with hunger. He felt like a man who'd been without water for days and was getting his first sip. In some corner of his mind, he knew he should slow down, shouldn't let her see how much he needed her, but it wasn't a matter of choice. It was a thriving, grasping instinct in his gut that reminded him of how desperate he was for her.

He slipped his tongue past her lips to familiarize himself with the secrets of her mouth all over again. Her breath caught and her hands fell to his shoulders as if she were holding on for strength.

He felt the clench of her slender fingers on his flesh, the tight tips of her breasts burrowing into his rib cage, and felt a sheen of perspiration on his brow. Every minuscule move from her body impacted him like an electric charge.

His mind shorted out, and for one glorious moment it was just Lisa, panting softly and taking all he could give. All sensation. Rocking against her, he lowered one hand to the small of her back and skimmed the other to her breast. Her nipple jutted against his palm, and suddenly it wasn't enough. "I want to feel your skin," he muttered into her neck.

Pulling her T-shirt loose, he ran his hands up over her waist and pushed past her bra to cup her full breast. At the first touch of his palm on her skin, his groan mingled with hers. He rolled the impudent nipple between his thumb and forefinger. With each caress, Lisa twisted against him, her shirt rising a little more with each movement.

His body tightening like an overstretched wire, he sucked in a breath of air and lowered his mouth to that pouting nipple.

Lisa's knees dipped. His tongue massaged her until she felt the tug in every one of her feminine recesses. It was as if her body knew what her mind denied. Everything Brick did was a call to mate.

He nudged her to the wall, trapping her in the hard circle of his body and arms. "I want your jeans off." He gripped her hips with his hands. "I want to touch your legs and spread them apart."

His words thrilled and shocked her. Lisa saw the blatant need in his eyes, explosive and mind robbing, and she wondered if after he kissed her again, there'd be anything left of her but ashes.

But then she didn't wonder anything, because Brick bent his knees and his full jean-clad arousal found a home between her thighs and his mouth took her around the world with a searing kiss.

Her scent was making him crazy, Brick thought. In his mind, his tongue was his sex and she was open, moist, and responsive. He thrust, and she cupped him with her tongue and lips. He rolled against her and she cuddled him with her thighs. Her bare breasts pressed erotically into his chest, and her hair whispered against his throat. But it was her scent that made him feel out of control, it grabbed his gut and heart and made his mouth bone dry.

He needed to breathe, needed to think, but his hunger for her was a freight train roaring at top speed. He wrapped his hands around her bottom and pumped against her in rhythm with his tongue.

Lisa whimpered and spread her legs.

Brick felt the first scorching rush. He swore. He wanted to be inside her for real, not just in his mind. His body needed the release. His body had been fooled into believing Lisa was slick, open, and naked.

He jerked at the force of his climax, and Lisa clung to him with hands that trembled. He tore his mouth from her and they both gasped for air. A breathless little moan escaped her lips, and for a sliver of a moment as he braced his forehead against the cool wall, he wondered if she'd been as caught up as he had. The physical evidence of his release, however, brought him to his senses.

He pulled back, and her hands tightened around the back of his neck.

"Oh, God, Brick . . ."

The plea in her voice grabbed his heart and squeezed. He sighed and held her close, enduring the torture and sweetness of her partially clad body. He stood that way with her in his arms for several moments until she seemed to catch her breath. Damning his rampant desire for her, he finally took a decisive step away. He felt like a rutting bull and didn't want to see the look of dismay or censure in her gaze.

"Brick—You—" Her hand on his arm stopped him midmotion, forcing him to turn and look at her. The expression in her green eyes was one of arousal and bewilderment. "I—" She broke off and shook her head as if she couldn't articulate her thoughts.

Brick could have articulated his, but the words probably would have scorched her ears. Still wrapped up in a ton of different feelings, he swallowed hard. "Don't try to say anything. Just give me a minute in here, and I'll meet you in the kitchen."

Her eyes were wide with confusion. "But—"

"Please," he said in a rough voice, and turned away.

Lisa stood in the hallway, staring for a full minute after he'd closed the bedroom door. Her legs threatening to give way, she leaned against the wall. Her equilibrium was shot and she felt like an emotional basket case, but she didn't call after him. She didn't try to tell him that her body was still buzzing with arousal, or that she'd nearly gone right over the top with him. She didn't try to tell him that touching him felt so good that it hurt. Most of all, she didn't tell him that she loved him. She wasn't sure he'd want to hear it and ultimately it didn't matter, because although Brick cared for her and was aroused by her, she knew he absolutely did not love her. At least, not enough to marry her.

The incident made her more cautious with him, Brick noticed a week later as they discussed the possibility of coordinating transportation to deliver unserved leftovers of some of Lisa's catered meals to homeless shelters in the area. When she'd insisted on meeting for lunch in a public place, Brick knew he'd lost ground, and he damned his unchecked response to her all over again.

She seemed friendly, but a little nervous. They'd managed, however, to firm up the arrangements, and Brick was determined to keep every mutual thread of connection between them.

Since he knew her work schedule, he made a habit of calling her during her off-hours every day to ask how she was and to talk. It was amazing what he learned in those conversations simply by listening. Her voice had the power to turn him on, but Brick concluded wryly that his body must have realized that *some* things simply couldn't be done over the phone.

With every conversation, he gleaned a new little fact about her. Like the fact that white roses were her favorite flowers, and that she kept a secret stash of fruit-flavored candy. She'd never gone "steady" with a guy in high school. The confession had made him want to dig out his high school ring. Steady he could do, marriage he could not.

He noticed that she often spoke of her family, leading him to believe they were very important to her. And she worried about her friends. She was a nurturer, he realized, and though he fought the reality, it was logical that a nurturer would want babies.

He wondered why the thought of babies didn't shake him as much as marriage did.

❖━━━━━━━━━❖

The phone rang later than usual on Thursday. Lisa had begun to think of her conversations with Brick as the one forbidden pleasure she allowed herself these days. Dates with a mission were such a drain.

She and Brick didn't usually discuss anything all that intense, but their little talks made her feel cared for. And since they were separated by miles, she didn't have to worry about doing anything foolish, such as asking him to kiss her again. Instead, she could just wish it, she thought darkly as she picked up the receiver.

"Hello," she said, expecting Brick on the other end of the line.

"Hi. Howyadoin?" he replied in a slurred voice.

Lisa frowned. "Brick? You sound strange. Are you okay?"

"Yeah. Just a little headache."

His words were running together. She felt a flutter of concern. "Are you sick?"

"No, no, no." He gave a long sigh. "You're not s'posed to be talkin' 'bout me. I called to hear about you."

Her heart twisted. "I don't want to talk about me. What's wrong?"

"Nothing, really, except for my head. Feels as if a demolition team got inside and stripped it."

"Have you been to the doctor?"

"Yeah. They gave me some medicine at the emergency room. That's probably why—"

"Emergency room!" she nearly shouted.

A long silence followed. "Lisa, please don't yell at me right now."

She took several deep breaths to stem the panic. "Why did you go to the emergency room?"

"S'not that bad. I took a little spill and scraped my head."

Lisa's gut instinct told her that Brick's definition of a little spill and hers were miles apart. "What did you fall off?"

He gave another heavy sigh. "A twenty-foot ladder, but I didn't get that many stitches, and, Lisa, you know how hard my head is."

Every new piece of information she pried out of him only made her feel anxious, and he was still running his words together.

"I've got my alarm set to wake me up every couple of hours, so—"

"I'll be over in ten minutes," she firmly interrupted.

"You don't need to. This'll pass."

Lisa felt a strange burning sensation behind her eyelids. She couldn't explain her relationship with Brick to anyone, let alone herself, but she knew she couldn't leave him alone after he'd been hurt. "Ten minutes," she said, and hung up the phone.

Brick winced at the loud click reverberating through his mind and gingerly lowered his head to the pillow. If he hadn't looked in the mirror an hour before, he would have sworn his head was the size of a watermelon. The doctor had preferred for Brick to remain at the hospital overnight, but Brick hated hospitals, so he'd used all his persuasive abilities to get released. His foreman had given him a ride home and promised to stop by later.

Brick had taken a shower, called Lisa, and now he was worn out. He would close his eyes for only a minute, he told himself. Lisa would be there soon.

Somebody was thumping the watermelon, he decided moments later. The pounding he heard seemed to penetrate his blood vessels and bones. A feminine voice called out, and he realized it was Lisa.

He dragged himself to the door and opened it. Everything seemed a little fuzzy to him except the concern he saw on Lisa's face.

She shook her head and entered the room. "Oh, Brick, you should be in bed." Dropping her purse on a chair, she set down a package that smelled suspiciously like chicken soup. She took his arm and gently guided him down the hall. "Come on. You have no business being up."

"I couldn't open the door from my bed," Brick grumbled, but allowed the fuss. Her scent swam around him, making him feel more dizzy than he already was, but it was a good kind of dizzy. He breathed in deeply. "Lord, you smell good. I'm buying a warehouse full of your perfume. What kind is it?"

His words were still running together, Lisa noticed. "Obsession," she absently answered, still nudging him toward the bed.

"That's me, obsessed." He stopped, feeling a momentary discomfort over her caring for him. "Waitaminute. Do you want something to eat or drink? I've got—"

"Would you please stop being polite? If I want something to drink, I'll get it. Right now I'm worried about you. I don't like the looks of those stitches. I don't like your color. And I don't like the way your sentences keep running together."

Brick hooked his thumbs in his belt loops and frowned. It was, she thought, the sexiest frown she'd ever seen. "Is there anything you do like about me?" he asked.

"Too much," she muttered to herself, taking in his appearance. True, he did look pale beneath his tan, and the doctor had obviously been forced to shave part of Brick's hair to put in the stitches. Compassion for those less fortunate could almost always be found in Brick's eyes. Lisa had learned that fact over the last year. His square jaw advertised his determination. And the strength of his body was revealed in shoulders that she would swear could withstand the weight of the world. The only burden he couldn't stand, she reminded herself, was marriage.

Yes, she admitted glumly, there was too much to like about Brick. She leaned closer to him and gently pushed at his broad shoulders. "Lay down," she whispered.

His eyes flickered with heat, and his lips tilted into a bad-boy grin. "You wanna help me?"

Lisa felt that unwelcome flip in her stomach again, and considered turning around and leaving until she saw his grin turn into a wince of pain. He sank down on the bed and groaned. "I'm completely at your mercy," he muttered, and slowly eased his head onto the pillow. "I've got you here in my bedroom, and I can't do a damn thing about it."

Lisa's lips twitched as she shifted his feet on top of the coverlet. "You don't need to worry. I won't do anything unseemly."

"That's a shame." He closed his eyes. "I prob'ly wouldn't remember it anyway, though."

Lisa ignored that statement. "What did the doctor say?"

"I'm supposed to wake up every hour till tomorrow," he said, his tone low and drowsy. "Don't get the stitches wet. Drink plenty of fluids," he recounted. "Rest." He gave a long, heavy sigh, as if he were exhausted. "I told you I feel like crap," he warned, his voice fading. "I think . . . I'll . . . goto . . ."

"Sleep," she finished for him, and checked the clock. In sixty minutes she would wake him. Lisa stroked his forehead, pushing a strand of his hair aside. His stubby eyelashes were light at the tips, she noticed, a result of all the time he spent in the sun. He looked like a rough-and-tumble boy who'd finally surrendered to the human need to sleep.

She wondered what kind of child he'd been. She wondered if he would ever have any rough-and-tumble sons of his own. Her heart squeezed at the thought. Brick didn't want the responsibilities of marriage and children, so she shouldn't grow accustomed to touching him, she decided, and pulled her hand away. She shouldn't let her mind dwell on him too often. And she should do her very best to get her heart back from him, so she would be able to give it to someone else.

After an hour had passed, she gently touched his shoulder. "Brick," she said. "Brick, wake up."

When his even breathing didn't change, she nudged him more firmly. "Brick, wake up."

His eyelids fluttered, and he lifted his elbow to shield his eyes from the bedside lamp. "Lisa?"

She felt a sliver of relief. "Yes, I have to wake you up. Remember?"

"Am I dreamin'?"

She smiled. "I don't think so. Want some ginger ale?"

He nodded and slowly pushed himself up to lean against the headboard. Accepting the glass, he drank down the iced beverage in nearly one gulp. "When my mom was alive, she always gave us ginger ale and graham crackers when we were sick."

"My mom gave us ginger ale and saltines."

"Yeah. My mom was fun, but sometimes she did some crazy things." He shook his head, and Lisa noticed his eyes were bleary. "Did I ever tell you that she wanted to be a country-music singer?"

Lisa shook her head.

"The urge hit real bad when she was pregnant with me. That's why she named me what she did," he said in a tone that indicated he still didn't believe it.

Lisa's curiosity was spiked. "What did she name you?"

"It's a secret."

"Oh."

He looked at her then, his gaze questioning. "You have to swear you won't tell."

Lisa lifted her hand in a silent oath.

He grimaced. "Elvis Pendleton."

Lisa stared at him in disbelief. A choked snicker escaped her throat. Her first instinct was to howl with laughter. When she saw the brooding expression on Brick's face, though, Lisa bit the inside of her cheek so hard, she wondered if she'd drawn blood. She cleared her throat. "I didn't think Elvis was considered a country-music singer." Her voice sounded unnaturally high to her own ears.

"That's what I told her," he said glumly.

Lisa could imagine a young Brick trying to correct his mother's point of view. Young Brick? Young *Elvis*. Her eyes burned with the effort she made to hold back an unladylike guffaw. "Your, uh, your family doesn't call you Elvis."

"Not if they want to live," he said in a mild, yet lethal voice. "The last time Troy did, he was six and I relieved him of his two front teeth."

"Brick, a hundred lines of Elvis songs are running through my mind," she confessed, contorting her lips to keep them from twitching wildly.

"Lisa," he said, his voice weary, "I've heard them all. You can laugh all you want after I go back to sleep."

"I guess that means you don't want me to sing 'Love Me Tender' for a lullaby."

EIGHT

Twenty minutes later Lisa stood in Brick's den and nearly burst her sides with the laughter she'd been holding back until "The King" went to sleep again. She wiped tears of hilarity from her eyes. The name certainly explained a few things. Now she understood why he'd gotten into so many fights as a youngster. She also guessed the origin of his nickname, since he'd adamantly refused to use his given name to the point of shedding blood over it.

Sniffing back another snicker, Lisa eyed those photo albums covetously. What she wouldn't give . . .

Absolutely not, she told herself as she marched toward the kitchen. She heated up the chicken soup instead.

As the night wore on, every time Brick woke

up, he told her something new about his family or himself. It was as if for a short window of time he was more vulnerable, more willing to disclose. She wondered if that was part of the reason he'd never stayed until morning with her.

Certain he would never have shared all this without the bonk on the head, she also wondered if he would regret it when he realized what he'd done. She cringed at the thought, but realized he probably wasn't going to be pleased.

When she woke him around three o'clock in the morning, he rubbed his face and shook his head from side to side. "I wish I had a dozen white roses for you," he muttered. "You're missing a whole night's sleep for me."

"It's no big deal," she protested, moved by the mention of flowers.

Muttering something unintelligible, he rolled to a sitting position and frowned. "It's nothing you've never seen before, but you might wanna turn your head." The warning was stamped across his face. "I'm ditching these jeans. I don't usually wear anything to bed."

Lisa froze as she watched him stand, unbutton, and unzip. He pushed the denim material down over his bare hips and thighs. Despite his injury, the beauty of his nearly naked body made her breath hitch in her throat. His broad shoulders tapered to narrow hips. A spray of brown hair on his chest was echoed in the nest that cupped his masculinity.

Brick had always seemed to give little notice to his impressive physique. Tonight was no exception.

Lisa, however, had always been extremely impressed by Brick's body. Tonight was no exception.

She drew a breath and made the quick prudent decision to leave his bedroom.

He lifted a hand to his forehead and swore.

Her prudent intention disappeared into thin air. "Sit down," she murmured, coming quickly to his side and kneeling.

"I'm tired of this headache," he growled.

Trying to keep her touch as impersonal as possible, Lisa pulled the jeans past his knees down to his feet. The hem was great for tucking into work boots, but a pain for pulling off. He lifted his foot, and she squelched the scandalous urge to tickle the sole. She must be getting punchy, she thought.

"Other foot," she told him, determined not to dwell on the fact that her head was inches away from his bare thighs. His musky male scent called to something inside her. Something best denied, she knew, and gave a sigh of relief when she freed his other foot from the jeans.

"There," she said brightly, and was about to stand, when Brick's fingers tangled in her hair.

"Lisa," he said in a night-soft voice.

"What?" She deliberately kept her gaze fastened on the camel-colored carpet.

He tugged at her hair. "Why did you come tonight?"

She closed her eyes against the emotions that swelled inside her. "You were hurt."

"So."

Lord help her, at this moment she didn't know how to fight him, how to fight her own feelings. She bit her lip. "I thought you needed someone."

"Anyone?" he prompted in that quiet male voice that tugged at her womb.

"I don't know," she admitted. "Maybe anyone." In a voice that sounded wispy and unsteady to her own ears, she confessed, "Maybe me."

A charged silence followed. Lisa felt as if there were a wire from Brick's will to her mind. Her mind bounded between should and shouldn't until she was utterly compelled to lift her head and meet his gaze. On the way to his eyes, she noticed that he was obviously aroused.

"This is crazy," he whispered harshly. "My head feels like it's splitting wide open. The only thing I should want to do is sleep off the pain." He swallowed audibly. "But seeing you down there, feeling your breath on my legs, and touching your hair . . ." He shrugged as if he couldn't explain it.

Lisa nodded because she understood completely. Perhaps it should have seemed that since she kneeled at his feet she was in a subservient role. Strangely enough it wasn't. For the first time since she'd known him, Brick was physically vulnerable. He'd never even had a cold when they'd been lovers. Now he was allowing her to help him, and Lisa knew that was significant.

She knew this was a rare moment. It made her eyes burn and her heart hammer wildly in her chest. She felt both powerful and humbled at the same time.

Her gaze traveled down his body, and shocking sensual images filled her mind. She experienced an overwhelming urge to press her lips to his rock-hard thigh. She wanted to rub her hair against him. She wanted to do things to him with her mouth that she'd never done before. The power of her desire made her tremble.

Lisa cleared her throat and tried to clear her mind. "You're hurting," she reminded him. "You should get back in bed."

"I don't want to go to bed by myself, Lisa." He lifted her hand and held it against his thigh.

His muscles were hard and defined and his skin was so warm beneath her palm. The combination of his inherent power and need was hard to resist when her blood ran like a fever through her veins. Yet the way his thigh trembled beneath her touch was what nearly undid her.

Oh, Lord, she silently begged for strength.

"Brick, I'm trying to do the right thing. Please don't make it difficult."

Brick's eyes smoldered with unspent passion as he allowed her to remove her hand. "Like I said earlier, I'm at your mercy."

It was one of the most difficult things she'd ever done, but she put a clamp on her imagination and desire. "Sit down," she whispered. "Let me get you some water."

Giving her a look that clearly said he wanted far more than water, he lowered himself to the bed. Trapped by his gaze, she slowly rose from her knees.

He crooked his finger for her to come closer.

Lisa shook her head. "No."

"Just one kiss," he said. "Just one little good-night kiss."

Lisa took a deep breath. "No."

Weariness shaded his face, and he sighed. "I promise we'll stop after one."

"You can promise that," she managed in a husky voice, her gaze sill locked with his as she backed toward the door. "But I can't."

For the rest of the night, Lisa was on guard. She woke Brick at appropriate intervals but ginger-ly kept her distance from him. The next morning in the clear light of day, Lisa decided that caring for Brick and being with him in the middle of the night had brought on some kind of temporary madness. One she vowed would not be repeated even though her stomach fluttered at the intimate look he tossed her way. He was much better this morning, she realized, so he wouldn't need her hanging around. The I'm-gettin'-under-your-skin-and-stayin' expression was on his face.

A quiet protective inner voice told Lisa to get out before she started making wishes that couldn't come true.

After fixing him a light breakfast, she began her good-byes. "You look as if you're feeling better now," she said as she picked up her purse. "If you need anything, just call and—"

"You don't have to go," he interrupted, his spoon midway between the bowl and his mouth.

"Oh, yes I do." This whole situation was too cozy, too appealing. "But, like I said, if you need—"

"Wait a minute." Brick frowned, putting his spoon down. He stood and hesitated as if undecided. "I want you to have something." He quickly disappeared down the hall and was back before she could demur. He came to a halt close beside her and handed her a small old box.

Her heart gave an odd little twist. "What is it?" She looked at him quizzically and started to lift the top off.

His hand covered hers. "Open it when you get home." He seemed both self-conscious and determined at the same time. "You need," he began, and shrugged as if that wasn't quite right. "There are—" He raked his hand through his hair and sighed. "Hell. There are some things you want that I can't give you, Lisa. You deserve to get everything you want." His gaze was full of honesty, but his mouth was set in a self-derisive, unhappy line. "I wish I could, but I can't. This is something small, but you said nobody had ever given you one, so I wanted you to have mine." He squeezed her hand. "And no matter what happens, I want you to keep it."

Lisa hadn't a clue what to say after that. She felt as if she'd been sucked into an emotional vacuum. She didn't know what was in the box, and after what he'd said she wasn't quite sure it mattered. She swallowed hard over the lump in her throat and scooted away from Brick. She could have kicked herself for being surprised. Suddenly noticing that he was waiting for her response, she nodded for lack of anything else to do. "Well, uh, thank you." She forced the corners of her lips upward and wondered why she felt so utterly sad. "I've got to go. You feel better, okay?"

"Yeah." He planted his hands on his hips and narrowed his eyes. "I appreciate your coming over last night and everything."

Shrugging, Lisa turned the doorknob behind her and pushed. "Isn't that what friends are for?"

Brick heard the faintest quiver in her voice and

felt a shot of alarm. She wasn't meeting his gaze. "Hey, I'll call you later." He reached for her arm, but she slipped beyond his reach.

At that moment Lisa had the look of a child held together by nerves and a prayer, and Brick had the sinking feeling that he'd screwed up again. "I'll call you," he repeated.

She pressed her lips together in a semblance of a sad smile. "Whatever."

Then she turned and walked away.

An hour later after she'd done a half-dozen things to distract herself from her curiosity, Lisa sat down on her floral couch and pulled the top off the box. For a moment, she simply stared at it. Then she lifted the silver piece of men's jewelry and held it in her palm. It was cool and heavy with an amethyst stone and was inscribed with the words *Beulah County High School, Class of 1980.*

Shaking her head, Lisa smiled and slipped the class ring onto her index finger. At another time in her life, she would have put that ring on a chain and worn it around her neck. At another time, she would have felt euphoric and proud to wear it. It would have been enough to hold her forever. Or at least until graduation, she amended wryly.

She rolled it back and forth between her thumb and forefinger. She wondered what had possessed him to give it to her, then struggled with a burning wave of embarrassment as she remembered her foolish confession a few nights earlier. She wondered if he'd ever given it to another girl.

Lisa rolled her eyes at the crazy thought. Was she really jealous over a high school romance Brick may have had?

Lisa stared at the ring and sighed. At another time it would have been enough for her, and Lisa was moved far more than she wanted to admit. But she wanted more than a ring, even if it was a diamond engagement ring, she realized. She wanted a man, marriage, and family.

Her throat knotted, and Lisa put the ring back in the box. It was such a little thing that it shouldn't have affected her so much. She told herself that over and over as the tears fell like warm rain down her cheeks.

The strength of her feelings for Brick frightened her enough that after she was assured he had recovered from the concussion, she made the decision to stop taking his calls.

The following Thursday at the office, Senada handed her an assortment of phone messages. "Two from Brick today," she said with a disapproving glance. "I thought you two were *fini*."

"It's a little more complicated than that," Lisa hedged, flipping through her calendar.

"It seems simple to me. You want to get married." Senada said the word with distaste. "I don't know why, but I accept that you do. Brick doesn't, so you dump him and find another man." Senada's lips lifted in a cynical smile. "There's always another man."

Lisa had often wondered what had made Senada so cynical about men, but her business partner wasn't inclined to discuss the subject. "It isn't that easy, Sin. I've known Brick for a year now, and since we've stopped—dating—" The word still seemed completely inadequate when used to describe their relationship. She sighed. "We've become friends. The problem is that it isn't always easy to separate the new friendship from all those old feelings."

Senada arched a dark eyebrow. "Isn't easy for whom?"

Lisa felt her cheeks heat. "It isn't easy for either of us," she admitted, remembering the strong emotional and physical pull that always seemed to hover beneath the surface. It threatened to erupt and overwhelm her every time they were together.

"You're still hot for him."

Lisa stiffened, feeling as if she'd taken a direct hit. She opened her mouth to deny, deny, deny, but the truth was a thorn in her side. She felt a depressing surge of defeat. "I'm trying not to be," she finally said in a low voice.

"Oh, *chiquita*." Senada shook her head in sympathy. "You want him, but you don't want to want him. Sounds as if you're stuck between a brick and a hard place."

Despite her ongoing frustration, Lisa's lips twitched at Senada's twisted version of the old cliché.

Senada picked up the two phone messages from Brick. "He obviously still wants you too. Maybe you can change his mind about getting married."

"No," Lisa said immediately, recalling the pain and humiliation she'd experienced the one time she'd confronted him with her need for a family. "I've already talked to him about it. It was a horrible experience, and I refuse to do it again. Especially," she continued, when it appeared that Senada was going to interrupt, "since I know he hasn't changed his views on marriage. He may have changed in some areas, but not marriage."

"If he changed his mind about one thing, then—"

"No." Lisa shook her head. "I felt like I was asking him to marry me. Do you know what it's like to be turned down for that?"

"No, but I know what it's like to be turned down for other things," Senada said thoughtfully. "How many times did I ask the Arts Council if we could do their Winter Ball before they said yes? More importantly, how many times did they say no?"

"At least a dozen," Lisa admitted, "but it's not the same thing."

"I *wanted* that Arts Council job with a passion." She flipped her dark hair behind her shoulder. "You've got to go after what you want. Pull out all the stops and go for broke. If you want Brick to be the father of your children, you shouldn't let a little two-letter word stop you."

That two-letter word held an enormous amount of power, Lisa thought. "I don't know."

Senada snorted. "Don't wimp out."

Lisa's temper lit. "It's not a matter of wimping out, Sin. I'll admit I'm scared. If things don't work out, I'm afraid I'll end up in pieces. If I go for broke and try everything I can think of to get Brick to change his mind about marriage, what happens if he still doesn't want to?"

Senada hesitated. "That's a problem. It's more of a risk for you than it would be for me, because I can't imagine wanting to marry a man that much." She shrugged. "If he still didn't want me, I'd probably tell him to go eat some dynamite." She gave a melodramatic sigh. "Then I'd check my Rolodex for someone else to comfort me in my hour of need." Senada made a face and squeezed Lisa's arm. "Sorry, *chiquita*. I don't think I'm helping very much. I think you're gonna have to roll your own dice on this one."

And that was the crux of the matter, Lisa realized later. She didn't want to roll the dice. She didn't want to wonder what would or could happen. She didn't want to guess how long he'd stay or when he'd go. She didn't want to play the game anymore. She wanted a sure thing.

"I'm sorry, Brick," Senada said, her voice patently insincere. "Lisa can't take your call right now. Would you like to leave a message?"

Brick swore under his breath. "Why should I leave a message when I know you're tossing all of them into the circular file?"

"How do you know *I'm* the one who's throwing away your messages?"

Her words cut to the very heart of him. "Lisa throws them away?"

"Oh, don't sound so wounded," Senada said in disgust. "Lisa's vulnerable right now. She doesn't need you bothering her."

He narrowed his eyes at the cold pain settling in his chest. "Is that what she said? Is that why she hasn't talked to me in over a week?"

"She's confused." Senada paused, and her voice softened. "I'm worried about her. She seems worse today. As if she's sitting on the edge and . . ."

His gut clenched. "And what?"

"I really shouldn't be discussing this with you, Brick. Especially since your intentions aren't honorable," she added in a meaningful tone.

"Give me a break, Senada. I've been trying to

talk to her for almost two weeks. You're not the only one who cares about Lisa."

"I'm not hurting her, though."

Brick looked at the ceiling and counted to ten. Senada's barbed comment was right on target, but he was wrestling with his own confusion and sense of loss. "You're probably not going to believe this, but I don't want to hurt Lisa. I want her to be happy. She's the most important woman in the world to me. I—"

"Then why don't you marry her?" she asked bluntly.

Brick's mind froze. He squeezed his forehead and swallowed hard. "It isn't that easy."

Senada gave a heavy sigh. "Lisa says the same thing."

"Then tell me what you meant when you said she seems worse today." When Senada remained silent, he ground his back teeth. "Please."

"It's really been for the last two days. I don't know what it is, but she seems like she's running on nerves. She's offering to cover extra jobs. She doesn't sit still for a minute, and she backed over a mailbox this morning. She's *working* at being cheerful."

The last statement was the most telling. Lisa didn't have to work at being cheerful. She was naturally. His uneasiness grew. "I need to see her. Where's she working tonight?"

"Absolutely not. What could *you* do to make her feel better?"

Brick absorbed the veiled insult without difficulty. His main concern was Lisa. He didn't really care what Senada thought of him. He was much more absorbed with his compelling need to see Lisa. For Pete's sake, it had been almost two weeks. "I could hold her," he simply said.

A long silence followed. He could practically hear Senada's inner struggle. "I hope I don't regret this," she muttered, and told him where Lisa was working.

Brick murmured a quick thanks and got off the phone. He decided to wait until her busiest time had passed and cooled his heels for three excruciating hours. He entered the hotel lobby armed with a bag of fruit-flavored candy in his pocket and a single white rose in his hand.

Minutes later, he found her in the kitchen with the other banquet staff where everything appeared to be winding down. Watching her from the doorway for a moment, he noticed that she looked tired, and as Senada had said, appeared to be running on nerves. She was so intent on her work, she didn't notice that he'd entered the room.

As Lisa leaned against the counter and scratched some figures on her inventory sheet, something flashed in her peripheral vision. She jerked her head up. A white rose held in a familiar strong hand was extended in front of her. She smelled the scent of the rose and felt Brick's body heat behind her.

"Surprise," he said in a low voice.

Her pulse immediately quickened. She studied the rose in silence. The gesture was touching, but it was the man who made her insides tremble. Since she'd gotten the news from her sister two days before, Lisa had felt as if she'd had the wind taken out of her sails. She'd hidden from her anguish with work. But now Brick was there and she suddenly felt vulnerable. She bit her lip and took the rose in her hand. "Thank you," she managed. "This is definitely a surprise."

"I wondered how you've been doing."

She closed her eyes and braced herself against a barrage of emotions. "I've been busy and I haven't taken your calls. I'm not sure I can explain, but—"

He cupped her shoulder, and she sensed he would have held her if they'd been alone. "You don't have to explain right now."

She sagged with relief. With the relief, however, her hard-won composure wavered. Brick's presence seemed to sharpen her senses, and her buried pain became fresher, more acute. She held her breath, willing the raw feeling to pass.

He gently turned her to face him, and she stood

for his inspection because she didn't have the energy to run or the desire to tell him to leave.

"I don't like the circles I see underneath your eyes," he muttered.

His concern made her throat close up. She swallowed hard. "You're not supposed to notice."

He scowled, but his eyes were gentle. "Let's get out of here. Can't you get someone else to finish up?"

"I could," she said, uncertain about the wisdom of leaving with him. "Where did you have in mind?"

Brick's gaze narrowed as if he'd guessed she was afraid to be alone with him in her apartment or his. He jabbed his finger toward the ceiling. "Up on the roof. The hotel has an observation deck."

It took only a moment to give instructions to her banquet coordinator, and Lisa and Brick were soaring toward the twenty-first floor in the elevator. The same elevator they'd been stuck in when Brick had turned her on with the tale of his fantasies about her. Fighting an insidious heat, she made herself focus on what the observation deck would be like: Scenic, the air would cool her face, and most importantly, the deck was *public*.

She hoped Brick wasn't going to be nice. She felt pathetically weak at the moment, and entirely too susceptible to his charms.

The doors whooshed open. "We're here," he said. His gaze met and held hers.

He didn't touch her, she noticed as she stepped from the elevator. He was being extremely careful. Good, she told herself, denying that she wanted his arms around her. Somebody needed to be careful.

Seeing no other visitors on the observation deck, Lisa walked as far as she could and wrapped her hands around the protective iron railings. The metal felt cool to her touch, and the breeze was warm due to the summer temperature. Buildings, lights, the shadow of mountains, and a million stars provided a panoramic view.

Brick stood next to her. "Bet it's pretty in the fall."

Lisa nodded. The back of his hand brushed hers, but he didn't lace her fingers through his. She had thought some of her excruciating inner tension would disappear when they stepped outside. Instead her awareness of Brick had heightened. She smelled his clean masculine scent in the breeze. She felt the warmth and strength from his body. Sliding a glance at him, she noticed his jaw was clenched, and his hand was in his pocket as if he were wound as tightly as she was. This was crazy, she thought, and was just about to suggest they leave when Brick pulled something out of his pocket.

"You want a fruit chew?"

Her favorite candy. The little kindness stripped her already shaky reserves, and the emotion of the whole week fell on Lisa like a wrecking ball.

"Oh, Brick," she wailed, and burst into tears.

NINE

At the sight of Lisa's tears, Brick automatically pulled her into his arms. "Lisa?"

His gut twisted when a shudder racked her frame. Alarm tore through him. Something horrible must have happened. He tightened his hold.

Lisa sobbed against his chest. "M-my sister—called m-me." Squeezing his shirt, she shook her head. "My youngest sis—" She sniffed and continued. "She's pregnant!"

Brick waited for the rest of the story, but Lisa sobbed again.

Certain there was more, he gently prodded her. "Is she okay?"

"Y-yes."

He stroked her hair in a soothing motion. "Is the baby okay?"

Lisa nodded.

Totally confused, he shook his head. "Then what?"

"I'm just so—so happy for her," she said, and another shudder racked her.

Every little sob turned him inside out. "Of course you are," he muttered as he rubbed her shoulders. He felt the warm wetness of her tears seep through his shirt. "Lisa," he murmured against her head. "Lisa, honey, you gotta tell me why you're so upset."

She took a deep breath and backed slightly away. Brick noticed that she seemed to be staring at his throat instead of his eyes.

"It's so stupid."

When he tilted her chin so she'd meet his gaze, she bit her lip. "What's so stupid?" he asked.

She squinted her eyes and another set of tears ran down her cheeks.

Brick wiped them away with his fingers. "Tell me."

"I'm happy for her, but I'm miserable for me," she whispered. "And I'm so ashamed."

Understanding hit him, and Brick felt a tug of empathy. "Aw Lisa." He pulled her back against his chest and tangled his fingers through the silk of her hair.

"What's wrong with me?" she asked in a shaky voice. "I just want a man to love me and a baby I can love. I realize that's not a very modern goal, but it's what I want."

His chest was heavy with her pain. "There's not a damn thing wrong with you." He gently shook her. "Do you hear me? Any man would—"

She lifted her head and looked at him with sad eyes. "Not any man, Brick. Not any man."

Brick's heart sank, and he swore in frustration. How could he explain to her that it was his problem not hers? Desperate to help her, he swallowed past the thick emotion in his throat. He put his hands on either side of her head and stared straight into her eyes. "I love you," he said gruffly. "I can't ask you to marry me, but I love you. I've never told another woman that. I realize it's just words and it may not mean much to you, but I love you."

He searched her gaze for understanding and died a little when he saw confusion. Knowing his words weren't enough, he took her mouth in a kiss that he hoped would say everything he couldn't.

She opened her mouth to his seeking tongue, and Brick filled himself with her sweet taste and the texture of her mouth. She clung to his shoulders and his body.

She kissed him back as if she were focusing the full range of her emotions on him. Her complete vulnerability stirred something primitive inside him. He tasted her sadness and fear, her confusion and desire, and it only made him want to make everything better for her.

Turning aggressive, Lisa pressed herself against him, her breasts to his chest, her abdomen nuzzling his arousal. Brick lost his breath while she sucked his lower lip into her mouth. She slid her hands down to his hips and pulled them into the cradle of her thighs.

His heart pounded with the fury of his leashed passion, his skin heated so that it seemed to sizzle where she touched, and he turned hard with the need to show instead of tell.

Everything was getting out of control. Brick tried to grab his sanity when she lowered one of her hands between them.

"Lisa! For God's sake." His body didn't want to stop her. It was too good having Lisa in his arms, having her hands on him again. It was too good and it had been too long.

He touched her breasts and she moaned with pleasure. Above the roar in his ears, he heard voices from the elevator. It took a moment for reality to kick in, a moment when Lisa wiggled deliciously against him. Brick closed his eyes and swore. He clasped his hand around her wrist.

"What is it?" she asked breathlessly. "Why did you stop me? Why—?"

Brick covered her mouth and stared into green eyes bright with arousal. "We're not alone anymore," he managed in a gruff voice.

He could see she was so aroused, she was edgy

with it. The knowledge did nothing for his self-control.

"I don't want to wait," she whispered, desperation written on her face. "I need you now."

She *needed* him. There was so much he couldn't give her that she needed, but, dammit, he could do this much. "Let's get out of here," he said, and tugged her toward the elevator.

When her legs failed her, he held her against him and stepped into the elevator. The door closed, he immediately took her mouth again, and the fury began as if they'd never stopped. She was all over him, her mouth on his, her hands pulling loose his shirt, her unique aroma wrapping around him like a scented satin sheet. In the mirrored walls, he caught blurred snatches of the reflection of her tousled hair, flushed cheeks, and her swollen mouth as she kissed his throat.

The multiangled sight of her was so sexy, he felt as if a blowtorch roared through his blood. Instinct took over. He wrapped his hands around her rear end and squeezed. Her flesh was warm, feminine, tempting. But he wasn't nearly close enough, so he slipped one hand beneath her skirt and thanked the Lord she was wearing thigh-high stockings.

Her lace panties were damp with her arousal. He slid his fingers underneath the edge to her core. She cried out.

That vulnerable, feminine sound made something inside him snap. "Do you want me now, Lisa?"

"Yes! Oh, Brick, yes."

He watched her eyes, huge with passion as he pushed the lacy triangle down her trembling thighs. Touching her hot, sweet femininity again, he felt himself swell painfully against the fly of his pants. "This is crazy," he muttered to himself, knowing the building would have to fall down before he would stop.

With his last bit of sanity, he pushed the stop button, halting the elevator between floors. He unzipped his pants, released his rigid masculinity, and picked her up. "I hope you're sure you want this."

"I'm sure," she said between uneven breaths as she wrapped her legs around his waist. "Give me you."

Give me you. He swore. It was too much. He pressed her against the mirrored wall and lifted her skirt. They took each other in one slick mind-robbing plunge. In the next seconds of spiraling sensation, Brick didn't know which breath was hers, which moan was his. He only knew she was the source of his every secret desire, his every hidden need, and she was milking him with tiny, exquisite shudders. She cried out, and he felt her clenching spasm.

For only a second he saw the rapture on her

face. Then he was gone, soaring after her into ecstasy.

Her forehead, damp with perspiration, pressed against his. Her eyes were shut and she fought for breath. "Oh, Brick—"

Brick was fighting for his own breath and equilibrium. "Give me a minute." Shuddering, he pulled away and allowed her feet to slide to the floor. She clasped his arms to keep from falling.

"Are you okay?" he asked, trying to make his mind work. They had to get out of the elevator.

She nodded, her eyes still dazed. "I—my legs—" She looked at him helplessly.

"Lean against the wall for a minute, honey." He kneeled down and with trembling hands gently pushed her hose and panties back up her legs, then put his own clothes back together. "I'm getting us a room for the night," he said, pushing the button for the lobby at the same time that he pulled her back into his arms.

Within five minutes, they were in the hotel room. Before Lisa could protest, he had her out of her clothes and in the shower. She was standing under the warm spray when he joined her.

Her hair was slicked away from her face in a wet curtain. Her skin was creamy with rivulets of water running down her throat to her breasts. Looking at her nipples made him want to put his mouth to them, then skim down her belly to the warmth between her thighs. The sight of her nudity brought a fresh surge of heat. He wanted her again.

"I can't believe we did that in the elevator," she said, wrapping her arms around him.

"Do you regret it?"

Her eyes dark with a woman's secrets, she slowly shook her head.

He sipped the water from her lips. "I feel like I've been living in a desert and you're the water I've needed for days."

"Oh, Brick." Her voice was a wisp of a sound, at odds with the wild craving he felt for her.

Feeling himself pulse to life, he lowered his mouth to her nipples, sipping each of them as he'd sipped her mouth. "Oh, Brick what?" he asked.

Closing her eyes, Lisa arched against him in pleasure. "If I'm the water, then drink up."

He did. Eager to rediscover and reclaim every inch of her, he took his time and devoted himself to the task. He was determined to get it right this time, to make sure he knew everything about her.

He watched her eyes dilate when he slowly grazed his thumb up her thigh to her sweet honeyed feminine secrets. He measured the depth of her shudder when he replaced his thumb with his mouth. He didn't miss a single soft whimper when he teased both of them by inserting just the tip of his aching erection inside her, then withdrawing.

The self-denial made his nerve endings agitate and his forehead prickle with perspiration. Still, he continued the sweet torture until he could stand it no longer.

What took his breath and stole his heart was the way she strained to hold back her completion until she was sure he was coming with her for the ride. She gently touched him, his cheek, his shoulders, his whole body, but he learned that it was the tenderness, not the technique, that made him feel so many things he didn't understand. He saw that his pleasure was just as important to her as her own was. It only made him want to please her more.

The night was full of their lovemaking. He didn't want a moment to pass that she didn't know the strength of his desire for her. He wondered how he'd endured the last two months without having her in his bed and in his life. At the same time, however, he wondered why he still felt the same resistance to marrying her. Every time he touched her, there lurked the dark possibility that it could be the last time. It could be his last drink of water. It fed his frantic pace until Brick and Lisa fell into an exhausted sleep at dawn.

Lisa's eyes fluttered open to the midmorning sunshine spilling through the gap in the curtain.

She immediately closed them. For such a little ray, the sun seemed obscenely bright.

She didn't look at Brick, but felt his presence beside her. His breath was slow and even, his body pressed to her side. There was no morning-after confusion. She didn't wonder where she was and how she'd gotten there. She remembered it all in vivid detail.

She remembered the exquisite sensation of having him inside her, how her slightest touch had excited him, and how he had rendered her speechless with his sensitivity. She remembered everything and refused to call something so wondrous a mistake. But she also remembered the driven desperation that darkened his eyes every now and then, and Lisa knew nothing had changed. He still couldn't tie himself to her. What made it worse this time was that it wasn't tormenting only her. It was obviously killing him too.

"Morning, Lisalove," Brick murmured in a sleep-husky voice.

Her heart twisted at the affectionate nickname. Turning to look at him, she took in the appealing sight of his tousled hair and the dark shadow of his bearded jaw. Then she stared into his violet gaze and struggled with a quick shaft of pain.

He propped himself on an elbow and bent over to kiss her, a long leisurely wake-up kiss that made her sigh when he pulled back.

She smiled. "Good morning to you."

He toyed with a lock of her hair. "You wanna have breakfast in bed? I can order something from room service."

It sounded wonderful. It would, however, prolong the inevitable. "I don't think so," she said, bringing the covers with her as she rose to a sitting position. She wondered where her clothes were.

"Not hungry?" He sat up, too, but didn't bother with the covers.

"No, I haven't looked at the time yet, but—" Lisa glanced at the alarm clock on the bedside table and shook her head. "Oh, my! Ten-thirty." Dismayed, she shifted her legs, and her feet touched the plush carpet. "You know how Saturdays are when I'm working. A million things to do . . ." Her voice trailed off when Brick fastened his hand around her wrist.

"Why are you in such a hurry to leave?" he asked in an even voice.

She took a deep breath. "I wouldn't call leaving at ten-thirty in a hurry."

"You just woke up."

Reluctantly she met his gaze. "It's time for me to go."

"Why?"

He shifted his shoulders, and she was suddenly aware of his masculine strength. It was amazing the way he attracted her with so little effort. She shook off the thought. "I mean, the night is over. It was an—" Searching for a word that could possibly describe it, she lifted her hand helplessly. "—an incredible night. A night I'll never forget. But the night's all gone now. We're the same people with the same minds, and our minds don't really agree."

His gaze darkened, and he began to rub his thumb over her wrist. "Our minds agreed last night. Everything agreed last night."

She couldn't dispute that. It was difficult to think with his finger making her pulse skip in time to his stroking. "But that was last night, and this is now. And I don't think our minds agree anymore."

"You're not saying you want to go back to us not seeing each other, are you?" Holding her gaze, he lifted her wrist and pressed his lips against her pulse.

Lisa's stomach jumped. It was a sensual, romantic gesture, the kind designed to make a woman leave her clothes on the floor and forget everything but the man. She wanted to. Instead, she stiffened her spine, refusing to give in to the nearly lethal desire he evoked in her. Pulling her hand away, she got out of the bed. "We can't continue sleeping together."

Brick was beside her before she'd grabbed a guest terry robe from the bathroom. "Why not?"

She tossed the other robe to him while she punched her arms through the sleeves of hers. She jerked the belt into a knot and placed her hands on her hips. "Because it hurts too much when it's over."

His robe dropped to the floor unnoticed. He put his hands on her lapels and trapped her with his gaze. "*Nothing is over.*"

Lisa's heart tripped over itself. She sighed. "Brick, we've been through this before. Don't make me go into it again. You don't want to marry me, and I need that kind of commitment. It hurts to make love with you when I know what's between us can't last."

He narrowed his eyes and didn't remove his hands. "Why can't it last when I love you?"

Lisa's breath stopped. He'd said it before, but she'd thought it was because of the heat of the moment. Now, in the light of day, it made something inside her wrench. Fighting confusion and sadness, she gave a tiny shake of her head. "Because I need something more."

Brick dropped his hands to his sides. His mouth twisted in cynicism. "You need a piece of paper, a ring, and a bunch of promises that most people break."

"Yes," she answered softly without apology. "I need all those things, but what I need more is the lifetime of working it out. Not everybody breaks those promises, Brick. Not everybody feels marriage is a prison." She looked at the ceiling in frustration. "Oh, why am I trying to explain it to you? I can't do this anymore." She picked up his robe and handed it to him. "Please put this on."

Brick shrugged into it and crossed his arms over his chest. "You keep saying you want to find another man to marry you, but when we get together, that doesn't seem too important. When I got that concussion, you stayed with me all night. I won't forget how you took care of me. And how you wanted me." His expression dared her to deny it.

She couldn't.

"Last night you said *give me you*." His voice was low and sexual. "When I touch you, you respond as if you belong to me and me alone, not some other man."

Lisa glared at him. "You're right," she admitted, lifting her chin. "You touch me, and I give you everything." Her voice began to shake. "My body, my heart, and my soul. And that's the problem." Lisa felt the first sting of tears in her eyes and blinked them away. "Every time we make love, I lose a little piece of myself because it can't last between us. We have a fundamental disagreement, and I refuse to try to trick you into committing yourself to me. I won't try to wear you down or talk you into it. It would be humiliating, and I respect you and myself too much to do it." Lord, this hurt.

She threw out her arms. "I know you care about me, but—"

"I love you," he interrupted in a deadly serious voice.

Every time he said it, it rocked her very foundation. She had to work to gather her composure. "You just don't get it, do you? Did you know that I have a hope chest in the back of my spare bedroom closet?"

He looked as if she'd hit him with a two-by-four. "No."

"Have you ever seen what a woman puts in her hope chest?"

He shrugged, looking wary and uncomfortable. "Not lately."

More like not at all, she thought. She could tell this was a disturbing subject for him. All the more reason for her to broach it. "Most women don't have hope chests anymore, but I do. That should tell you something about me, Brick."

She counted off the contents of her chest on her fingers. "I have sterling silver that my grandmother gave me, a quilt my mother made for me, and a hand-crocheted afghan my aunt made a year before she died. I have china. Pillows I embroidered when I was twelve, and the tackiest pot holders you can imagine. I made those when I was eight." She smiled in wry remembrance at her novice efforts. "There are sterling silver picture frames, and a baby blanket." She saw the dismay on his face and felt her smile fade. "You say you love me, but all this is part of me. In some very important ways, I guess I'm an old-fashioned girl." She clutched the collar of her robe. "I'm more than Lisa the catering manager or Lisa the lover with birth control pills."

Brick swore. "I never thought of you that way." He raked his hand through his hair and looked at her moodily. "But hell, I didn't know you had a hope chest."

He sounded horrified. If she didn't feel so bad, it would be funny. But nothing seemed funny to her right now.

Sliding one hand to his hip, he cocked his head to one side and studied her for one long, tension-filled moment. Lisa saw the instant the light dawned and felt her mouth go dry in trepidation.

"You're trying to scare me off with this story about a hope chest," he concluded in an annoyed voice. He shook his head, and a hint of a dangerous chiding grin tilted the corners of his mouth. "What is it, Lisa? Are you trying to use this talk of marriage against me the way you'd use a cross to fight off a vampire?"

"If the shoe fits," she retorted.

He leaned closer to her, his energy potent and consuming, his jaw set in determination. "Hope chest or not, I still want you. And you still want me."

The absolute truth of the statement frightened her. He wasn't being egotistical. He was simply stating a fact. "It's some crazy instinct that makes me want to turn to you, Brick, but it's an instinct that's hurting both of us." She shook her head. "I can't do this anymore."

Brick's eyes flashed with pain. "Yes, you can. Follow your instincts."

Feeling hollow and brittle inside, Lisa bit the inside of her cheek. "Not anymore."

The rest of the weekend Brick felt as if he'd been emotionally gutted. God, he hurt like hell, and there was no panacea for the pain. He wasn't a big drinker, so he couldn't get drunk. Thoughts of Lisa were so relentless, he couldn't sleep. At the moment he didn't give a flip about work. He knew he would later, but right now giving his heart and soul to the company held no appeal. The only other option was to visit his family in Beulah, but Brick couldn't bear the prospect of trying to answer questions about Lisa. Especially since he didn't have any answers himself.

Every time he asked himself why he couldn't marry her, he experienced the same intense physical reaction. It was almost as if he were allergic to the very thought. His mouth turned to dust, his heart palpitated, and his stomach rolled.

The possibility that he could have a phobia of marriage settled insidiously in his mind. Could it be? Could it possibly be?

The notion tormented him until Monday afternoon when he took a deep breath and decided to do something about it. The following afternoon Brick found himself in a place where he'd never dreamed he would set foot—a psychologist's office.

TEN

The middle-aged man who greeted him didn't look like Dr. Freud. He was a little round, clean-shaven, and quietly friendly.

"Sit anywhere you like," Dr. Michaels said, as he picked up the notepad off his desk.

Warily eyeing the couch, Brick sat in one of the two green cushioned chairs. He rested his ankle on the opposite knee, resisted the urge to drum his fingers, and felt self-conscious as hell.

Dr. Michaels sat in the other green chair and gave him an encouraging smile. "People often feel uneasy the first time. That's understandable. Maybe if you'll remember that my job is to help you, you might relax a little." He glanced down at the form Brick had completed. "I see here that you have some anxiety about marriage. Maybe we can start with you sharing your ideas about what marriage is like. What have the marriages in your family been like."

Surprisingly, Brick felt some of the tension ebb from his body. It helped to have a question to answer. He leaned back in the chair and started with his first memories of his parents' marriage.

When Brick drove home after the ninety-minute session, he felt exhausted, but less defeated. It had been a relief to get his thoughts about his parents and his stepmother off his chest. With the psychologist, he hadn't felt like he'd needed to soften the truth, as he often did with his brothers and sister.

He stepped into his apartment and felt a sense of change. It was subtle. He made himself think about getting married and still wanted to throw up. Discouraged, he scowled. Then it hit him hard. He wanted to change, and he wanted it done instantly. Prest-o, change-o, and Brick Pendleton was the Lord of all he surveyed.

He was suddenly impatient with this fear, gamophobia, or whatever the hell it was. It was getting in his way, he thought as he pulled a bottle of ginger ale from the fridge. He took a long pull from the soda and the taste reminded him of the last time Lisa had been there with him. His chest ached with a yawning sense of loss. His fear was keeping him from what he wanted. It was keeping him from Lisa.

With the same single-minded intensity he used in planning a difficult "shot," Brick set his mind to exorcising his own demons. Dr. Michaels was a short-term, problem-oriented therapist, and by the third session, Brick had a strategy. Abiding by Lisa's wishes, he hadn't called her since that morning in the hotel. He knew, however, that she was going on that blasted singles cruise, and Brick had every intention of testing his new strategy on the open sea.

Watching the merrymaking of the other cruise passengers as the ship departed Miami, Lisa leaned against the railing and wondered for the fifteenth time if this was the right move to make at the right time. Hearing a woman's coy titter, she winced. It felt distinctly wrong.

She'd almost canceled her reservations after that unforgettable night with Brick. If Senada hadn't kept after her, she probably would have. As it stood, Lisa had a suitcase of clothes she wouldn't normally wear. Beneath her buttoned, oversized jacket, she wore a sleek green halter sarong-style dress that showed off her cleavage and revealed a significant stretch of her left thigh. Another one of Senada's suggestions. Lisa had no intention of removing the jacket.

Instead of moping and hiding, she was supposed to be checking out the action, as Senada would say, and flaunting her thirty-eight-inch hips. She shouldn't be pining for a man who turned green at the mention of marriage. She shouldn't be wondering why he hadn't called her. She should be thankful that he hadn't.

She should attempt to have a better attitude, Lisa thought. After all, she could end up meeting a wonderful man who wanted to get married and have a family. Mustering a pleasant expression, she turned away from the railing, determined to make the most of the cruise.

As the ship rocked in a southerly direction toward the Bahamas, Lisa carefully wove her way through the crowd toward the pool area, where the staff served rum punch while a steel drum provided background accompaniment. A huge banner fluttered across the deck—Meet Your Mate, Not Just A Date.

"Looking for some of this," a very familiar deep voice said as she drew closer to the bar.

Lisa jerked around, searching the crowd for his face. It couldn't be, she told herself. It simply couldn't be Brick. He wouldn't be caught dead on a singles cruise, she thought, shaking her head even as she spotted him. There he was in the living, breathing flesh, offering her a plastic tumbler of punch. Numbly accepting the cool drink, she stared at him. The wind gently brushed his hair across his forehead. His gaze was warm and amused. His smile would have scared the sharks.

A flood of sheer panic jolted her out of her

daze. "What are you doing here?" she demanded.

His insufferable grin widened. "I'm here to meet my mate," he said around a poorly muffled chuckle.

Lisa narrowed her eyes. "And I just won the million-dollar lottery." She looked at the people milling around. "This is for people who are serious about *getting* married, not avoiding it. How on earth did you get past the agency screening?"

Brick shrugged. "I filled out an application. The secretary said they can always use more thirty-something men."

"I don't believe this." She took a generous gulp from the rum punch. The whole purpose of this exercise was to get away from Brick's influence and meet other men. She felt a shot of desperation mixed with anger. "You shouldn't be here. I don't know why you came—" She held up a hand when he opened his mouth to speak. "And don't give me that crock about your looking for a mate."

"How do you know it's a crock?" he asked, looking at her intently.

Lisa was so angry, she almost couldn't breathe. Her hands itched to dump the remainder of her drink over his gorgeous head. In fact, if there'd been more left, she might have done it. "Because you've repeatedly told me how you feel about marriage," she hissed. "This is the worst trick you've ever pulled, the very worst," she said emphatically.

"To show up here and *pretend* that maybe you've changed."

His face was utterly serious. "Maybe I'm not pretending."

Her heart seemed to stop. Then her brain kicked in. *This was Brick.* She took another drink and licked her lips. There was too much emotional water under the bridge between them. Too many times when she'd hoped for change and been disappointed. Too many times when she'd wished and been denied. The ups and downs had taken a toll on her, and right now, she felt as if she'd been pushed right over the edge. "Maybe," she said in a controlled, deliberate voice, "I don't believe you." She turned around and walked toward the bar.

She heard his oath and the sound of his footsteps coming after her. "After all we've been through, after all we've meant to each other, the least you could do is give me a chance."

"No," she said to Brick, and asked the bartender for another rum punch. "I'm going to have a good time on this cruise." She was more determined than ever. "I'm going to meet men. And I'm going to pretend you're not here. I'm going to ignore you."

Brick positioned himself directly in front of her. "When have we ever been able to ignore each other?"

Lisa swallowed over the lump forming in her

throat. The way he stood and his rough tone of voice seemed to reflect everything they'd been together, emotionally and sexually. "Good point," she conceded. "I guess this calls for drastic measures." Lisa unbuttoned the oversized jacket, pulled it off, and headed into the crowd.

Brick stared after the curvy feminine vision in green and fought the urge to howl. He cracked his knuckles instead. The incredible irony of the situation was enough to drive him nuts. Here he was ready to try to get past this gamophobia. He'd already made a good strong start, and Lisa not only didn't believe him, she planned to ignore him. He swore in frustration.

"Hi. I'm Kelsey Richards from New York."

Brick reluctantly tore his gaze from the other side of the deck where Lisa was creating a mass attack of whiplash among the male passengers. He glanced at the petite blonde beside him. "Hi, Kelsey. I'm Brick and I've already met my mate." He pointed toward Lisa.

Kelsey arched her eyebrow. "She doesn't appear committed."

Brick saw the men begin to swarm around Lisa like a pack of salivating dogs. He dug an antacid out of his pocket and popped it into his mouth. "She's just having a memory lapse."

Kelsey looked doubtful. "Well, if you change your mind . . ."

"Thanks. But I won't be changing my mind." His mood turned more grim as he realized he'd be too busy trying to change Lisa's mind.

Brick spent the rest of the afternoon finagling a seat at Lisa's table for meals. He discovered the location of her cabin and checked the cruise itinerary.

At dinner she shot him a hostile look, greeted him, then promptly ignored him in favor of the sales rep from North Carolina. She wore a soft-looking, clingy coral dress that he'd never seen before. Her brown hair fell in a lustrous mass of waves to her shoulders. She looked like a sumptuous feminine dessert that every man within shouting distance would want to sample. Watching her with a brooding sensation in his gut, Brick wondered if it would have been easier if he'd sat at another table.

As the meal wore on, however, her sparkling demeanor waned, and she surreptitiously pushed her plate away. "Is the ship rocking more than it was?" A frown creased her brow. "I didn't notice the movement as much as I do now."

The sales rep nodded. "They really haul it on the first night out and the last night back. If you're going to get seasick, you usually get it the first night. You look a little green around the gills. You want me to walk you back to your cabin?"

Over Brick's dead body. The guy obviously

wanted to do a lot more than walk her to her cabin. Brick carefully watched Lisa's response. Offering a weak smile, she shook her head. "No, I think I can manage by myself this time." She gave a vague, general good night, rose to her feet, and took a weaving, unsteady course through the dining room.

Sighing, Brick threw down his napkin and followed her.

Lisa spotted him after she took her key from her bag. Her skin was pale and she was taking deep breaths. "Go away. I don't feel good."

"After I make sure you're okay," he assured her, and pushed open the door. "How much rum punch did you have today?"

She made a face and lifted her hand to her head. "Four. I think I should have stopped at three."

"Try two," he corrected, and helped her toward the bathroom when she clutched her stomach and made a sound of distress.

Lisa stumbled into the tiny room and slammed the door behind her. Hearing her muffled heaving, Brick leaned against the wall. This could end up being a long night for her, he thought, feeling a tug of sympathy.

After a few minutes, she came out of the head, shaken and still pale. "I'm not your responsibility. You can go now."

Her easy dismissal made him grind his teeth.

"That's a matter of opinion. Do you want to get a shot at the clinic?"

Kicking off her sandals, she shook her head and eased onto the bed. "I want to lay down in a cool, dark, quiet room and pretend I'm on solid ground."

It seemed as if she wanted to pretend a lot of things, he thought darkly, remembering that she also wanted to pretend he wasn't there. He dampened a washcloth with cold water, wrung it out, then gently put it on her forehead while she lay with her eyes closed.

Her eyes opened, wide, green, full of emotions he couldn't read. "Thanks," she said in a husky voice.

Sitting down on the edge of the bed, Brick gave her a wry half smile. "You're welcome. Want something to drink?"

She gave a little shake of her head and lifted her hand to adjust the washcloth. The movement pulled the material of her dress tautly across her breasts and hiked her dress another couple of inches up her thighs. Even when she wasn't feeling well, she made him want her. It would feel so natural to lay down beside her.

He cleared his throat at the slow, sweet surge of arousal. "Nice dress."

"Senada's idea."

"Wanna take it off?"

Lisa blinked. "Wha—"

"So you can get more comfortable," he said quickly, although he had to admit it was the kind of a dress that made *him* want to take it off.

A look of skepticism crossed her face. "Maybe later." The ship rocked noticeably stronger and she blanched.

Distracted by her momentary fragility, he pushed a damp strand of hair away from her face.

Lisa took a careful breath. "I want you to stop being kind."

Brick raised his eyebrows. "Why?"

She frowned. "Because it's hard for me to stay angry at you, and I *am* angry at you. You didn't call me for two weeks, then—"

"You told me not to call you," he reminded her, pleased as hell that his telephone absence had bothered her.

Her frown deepened to a glare. "Then you show up on a cruise where I'm trying to meet other men. You have a—"

He flipped the washcloth over. "You don't need to meet other men. You're in love with me."

That statement took the wind out of her sails for at least three seconds. She gaped at him, then propped herself up on her elbows. "Well, I'm trying to change that!"

Brick gently pressed her shoulders back down on the bed. "I'm here to make sure you don't change it. You can check out the other men, talk and laugh with them, but it's me you want to be with."

"Your ego is as big as you are," she told him in a furious voice.

Brick gave a self-deprecating laugh. "Lady, my ego's taking the beating of my life. This goes deeper than a gut feeling."

Her expression changed in a heartbeat. She looked scared, and Brick felt a twist of compassion for her. God knew, he understood fear.

"I want you to stay away from me," she whispered.

"No chance," he whispered back.

"I'll tell everyone your name is Elvis," she threatened.

"I'll tell all those yuppie types you can't drive backward without running over something. They'll consider your auto insurance premium a heavy liability."

"That's unforgivably low." Her voice trembled.

Brick looked at her with cool, calculating eyes. "I'll go as low as I need to."

"Why?" she asked desperately. "This is useless, crazy. Why?"

He gently cupped her jaw and knew what he was about to say might sound arrogant and possessive, but he wanted her to know the full measure of his desire for her. It was more than desire, though, and greater than passion. She was as essential to him as oxygen, more important than food, as vital as water. He needed her to know. "Because you're mine," he told her in a quiet but firm voice. "And I intend to keep you."

Lisa told him where to put his intentions and threw him out. Her nausea evaporated under the heat of her fury. Still shaking with anger five minutes later, she looked for something to throw at the door of her cabin.

"Of all the *nerve!*" she yelled at the walls surrounding her.

She needed to vent in a very bad way. When she'd first seen Brick on board the previous day, the ship might as well have flipped upside down. That's what had happened to her heart. She'd missed him so much, struggled with a terrible sadness after she'd left him at the hotel. She'd barely managed to pull herself together, and there he was showing up again where she least expected him and putting every other man in the shade.

Lisa was beginning to suspect that no matter what she did, she wasn't going to be able to get rid of Brick. Even if she moved to another planet, she feared he would always be there in her mind and heart. The notion made her want to scream.

The sense of dread that had rumbled deep inside her threatened to burst to the surface. Taking a deep breath, she stood in the middle of the cabin with the ship rocking beneath her and felt the back of her neck grow damp with perspiration.

What if she couldn't shake him? What if she was in love for good with a man who couldn't or wouldn't marry her?

Needing comfort, Lisa wrapped her arms around herself. Her mind immediately flew to Brick and how his arms felt around her, how his fingers clasped her rib cage with a gentle grip. He wasn't in the room, but she could smell his scent. A flush of heat spread through her. The mere memory, the mere thought of him made her heart contract. She had grossly underestimated his hold on her.

Brick was in her blood, and she had never felt so hopeless.

The next morning Brick looked over the crowd of singles with an appraising eye. Lisa had ignored him at breakfast again. It was a nervous kind of ignoring. Brick considered that a slight improvement, but not quite enough. She was doing her best to stay focused on other men, so she wouldn't have to deal with him. Of course, Brick wanted Lisa to deal exclusively with him.

There was a contract that specified such exclusivity, and Brick was willing to try it with Lisa.

Marriage.

The familiar uneasiness immediately assailed him. An edge of panic crept in. His stomach churned, and he opened a new roll of antacids. He felt the strongest urge to cut and run, to say to hell with this.

But he didn't.

The sun reflected on the deep blue ocean making it sparkle like diamonds. Voices hummed around him. Brick took a deep breath and counted to twenty-five. He took another deep breath and counted to twenty-five, and repeated the anxiety-reduction technique another time.

A fraction of the tension eased. Brick felt a slow grin build from within. It had worked. His sessions with Dr. Michaels had accomplished several things, the most important of which was providing Brick with ways to cope with his phobia of marriage. Dr. Michaels called them coping skills. Brick called them his little bag of tricks, and although he hadn't completely overcome his fear, he knew he'd come a long way.

The secret, he'd learned, was to wait it out by using one of these little tricks. Brick wanted to propose to Lisa and try to explain about his fear, but he still felt leery of admitting such a weakness to her. Although he believed Lisa loved him, the idea of exposing himself that way made his skin crawl. Maybe it was foolish, but he didn't want her to think less of him. She was too important to him.

Shoving his hands into the pockets of his khaki shorts, he swore under his breath. It was hell trying to talk marriage to a woman who wasn't speaking to you. He needed to get her alone without any distractions, he thought, throwing a dark glance at a group of married wannabes swimming in the pool. He needed her to turn toward him instead of away from him. He needed her to drop her guard.

Brick accepted a cup of juice from a server and reviewed his options. He could lock her in his cabin until she agreed to listen. After her vehement response to his possessive statement the night before, however, he supposed that might not work so well. No, he needed her to turn to him out of her own free will. He thought of the variety of men who were on the cruise, many of whom he knew wouldn't appeal to Lisa. *Thank God.*

A wicked idea came to mind. Brick immediately rejected it. It was underhanded and dirty, not particularly fair. He couldn't do it. It wouldn't . . . At that moment, he caught sight of Lisa making her way to the pool area, wearing a bathing suit designed to raise the temperature of every man to steaming hot. Probably another one of Senada's damn ideas. Restraining the urge to throw a towel over her, he ground his back teeth and recalled that he'd told Lisa he'd go *as low as he had to* to keep her.

Temporarily forcing his attention away from

her, he surveyed the crowd again and reconsidered that wicked idea. There were men of all ages represented from various parts of the country. It took only a moment before he identified the first candidate who would send Lisa leaping into his arms.

ELEVEN

It was enormous work projecting calm on the outside when you were sweating a river on the inside. Lisa's doubts and uncertainties had only multiplied over night. She'd forced herself to focus on another man at breakfast, but she hadn't a clue what he'd said, and he'd talked for fifteen minutes straight. Thank goodness the man had been too self-absorbed to notice.

Even now, she felt Brick watching her. The realization started with a little tingle at the back of her neck and spread quicker than the fever from a common cold to every region of her body. Out of the corner of her eye, she noticed the silhouette of his athletic body. The sun glinted off his hair as it fluttered across his forehead. She could imagine running her fingers through the strands, relishing the crisp texture. She could imagine his breath on her face just before he kissed her. She could imagine him pulling her into an embrace so that her breasts meshed with his chest.

When her breasts began to swell, Lisa bit back a groan and mentally chastised herself. She tugged at her tiny bathing suit strap and wished she hadn't let Senada talk her into this. Silently cursing in frustration, she decided to skip lunch and remain by the pool until the ship docked at the island. Selecting a chair, she reminded herself she had a lot to be thankful for. The weather was gorgeous with not a cloud in sight. A lovely ocean breeze diffused the heat of the sun, and the atmosphere among the cruise guests seemed less frenzied today. Her seasickness had vanished. Lisa reclined in the chaise lounge and opened her book on getting married. She lamented the fact that the SPF 25 sunscreen she wore might protect her skin from the sun, but it wouldn't do a thing for the hot, achy feeling Brick's intent gaze caused inside her.

Two hours later, she was ready to throw herself overboard. She almost couldn't believe the odd assortment of men who'd hit on her during the last one hundred and twenty minutes. The first one, older than her father, had slyly called her *kitty cat*. Lisa's stomach hurt when strangers called her animal names. The second man indicated his preference for tall, curvy women in the same breath that he said his mother had also been tall and curvy.

They blurred together after that. Just when she recovered from one, another would approach her. She wondered if she were wearing a sign, *Weirdos, hit on me.* Thank goodness it was nearly time to dock.

Refocusing her mind on a scenic trip to the island, Lisa swung her legs over the side of her chaise lounge and slid her feet into her sandals. She put her unread book into a bag.

As she rose to leave a man with a ten-gallon hat slowed his heavy-booted stroll and stood directly in front of her. "Howdy, ma'am. I'm Cal Jeffreys from Iowa. Pleased to make your acquaintance."

Not another one. With great trepidation, Lisa placed her hand in his and tried not to cringe at his overly firm handshake. "Lisa Ransom from Tennessee. Thank you."

"I signed up for this cruise to meet a good woman."

She smiled carefully. "I hope you find what you're looking for."

He nodded. "You look like a good, sturdy girl," he said, eyeing her up and down appreciatively. "Not too scrawny like most of these other ones. I want a woman with meat on her bones."

Lisa blinked. She *guessed* this was his version of a compliment. Unable to think of a single suitable reply, she nodded vaguely.

"I've got me a farm, good livestock, and a new

truck." His chest swelled with pride. "Now, all I need is a filly to share it all with."

She refused to believe this could happen to her twice in one day. He was not calling her a horse, she told herself. Nevertheless, her stomach seemed to turn. "You need a horse?"

Cal gave a loud bark of laughter. "Good sense of humor. That's something else I like in a woman. You're pulling my leg, aren't you? When I say filly, I mean I need a bride who'll give me six or seven sons." He gave her a broad wink and tipped his hat. "I gotta check out the rest of the stock, if you know what I mean. But I'll keep you in mind."

Lisa stared after him as he left. *He'd called her a filly.* "Heaven forbid," she muttered under her breath, and decided she needed some Alka-Seltzer.

After an afternoon and evening spent exploring the streets of Freeport alone, Lisa fell into an exhausted sleep, dreaming of kittens and fillies. Some might call it overreacting, but she was so disgusted, she tossed the how-to-get-married book in the trash. She awoke with a strong desire to avoid any of the men she'd met at the pool, so she took the shuttle to the International Market. She walked out of a jewelry store and ran into Brick.

"Hi," she said, feeling an indecent rush of pleasure.

"Hi yourself." He crossed his arms over his chest and leaned against a wooden beam that displayed the sign for the market. His eyes lit with warm interest. "Enjoying the sights?"

Strangely embarrassed, she shrugged. "Uh, yes. It's beautiful here." She lifted her bag. "I've been shopping."

Glancing at the bag, he nodded. "Find anything interesting?"

"Just some odds and ends, a few pieces of jewelry."

"Haven't seen you lately."

"I wanted to get in as much sight-seeing as possible." It sounded lame to her own ears, but she was thankful that he didn't call her on it.

"Oh." He lifted an eyebrow. "Met anyone interesting?"

Lisa grimaced at the memory of the men she'd met the day before. She saw a hint of amusement flicker across his face. He replaced it with a guileless expression. Suspicious, she paused before she answered. "I think it's safe to say they were interesting. Why do you ask?"

He shrugged. "Just curious. I saw a couple of guys stop by your chair when you were at the pool yesterday. With the bathing suit you were wearing, it was a wonder you weren't mobbed," he finished with a slight edge to his voice.

"Senada picked it out. Two of the men called me

animal names," she confessed, and sighed. "That's one of those things I can't tolerate. I don't know why, but it just makes me crazy when men who don't know me call me pet names."

He smothered a chuckle and leaned closer. "No explanation needed. You don't call me Elvis. I won't call you animal names." He checked his watch. "Have you eaten yet? I'm going snorkeling in about an hour."

A shot of excitement and envy surged through her. "Snorkeling! I've always wanted to—" She quickly covered her mouth.

"You could go and ignore me," he suggested in a neutral tone.

Lisa felt her foolish words come back on a wave of embarrassment. "I'm not that good at ignoring you," she murmured, not pleased, but unwilling to lie anymore.

An edge of sensual ruthlessness flashed across his face and was gone. All she could do was deal with her own underlying uneasiness. A slow grin tugged at the corners of his lips. "Then you could go and not ignore me."

Her heart picked up the pace, and her mind waffled. She was on a cruise and she was tired of struggling with herself night and day. Why shouldn't she enjoy herself for one afternoon? For Pete's sake, it was only snorkeling, and she dreaded going back to the ship. What if she ran into one of those characters she'd met at the pool yesterday. "I don't have my bathing suit with me."

"You could buy one," he returned, overcoming the objection with ease.

"I wanted to stop by a linen shop."

He shot her an I-dare-you look. "We've got forty-five minutes."

Lisa didn't know if she was sinking or flying. "The ship leaves this evening. We'll need to get back in time," she told him, subtly reminding both of them that this little armistice ended at sundown.

He must have sensed her capitulation because he took her arm. "Where's this linen shop?"

On the way, she stopped in a little hole-in-the-wall place that sold everything from jewelry and sunscreen to swim wear. She selected a purple racing suit, Brick gave a nod of approval and they were off.

The linen shop carried lovely embroidered tablecloths. She could picture her table dressed in one of them with matching cloth napkins, sterling silver flatware and exquisite crystal. Rubbing the crisp fabric between her fingers, she added a candlestick and a man with violet eyes to the image.

Lisa groaned.

"Which one do you want?" Brick asked, brushing his fingers over the same cloth she was touching.

"I don't know. I love the red rosebuds on this,

but that Christmas one," she said, pointing to a tablecloth on display. "The detail on it is exquisite." She moved over to the display. "See the little gift boxes and children's toys." She touched each one as she named them. "The jack-in-the-box, the rocking horse, and rag doll."

"There's a toy train too."

More undecided than ever, Lisa pushed her hair behind her ear. "The rosebud one is more for general special occasions," she said, still looking at the Christmas cloth. "I usually go home for Christmas, so I don't know when I'd use it. It's something you'd expect someone with a big family to use. I guess I could get it for my mother."

But she didn't want to. Brick could hear it in her voice. He also heard something else, something Lisa wouldn't dream she was revealing. She wanted a family. It amazed him that her desire for a family would show up even in her choice of linens. It amazed him, but it touched him too.

"Get the rosebud tablecloth," he suggested, watching her carefully. "I'll get the Christmas one for you."

Turning to look at him, Lisa shook her head. "No. I wasn't hinting. I—"

He put his thumb over her lips. "I know you weren't hinting. I want to get this for you." He would have left it at that if he'd given in to the uneasiness crawling up from his gut, but Brick knew it was time to take another step forward. He drew in a deep breath, knowing this was just the beginning of laying his cards on the table. "I want to get it for your hope chest."

Lisa's heart seemed to stop. The room tilted. She stared at Brick, her jaw moving, but no sound coming out. She closed her mouth and swallowed hard over the lump in her throat. "Did you say hope chest?" she asked in an unsteady voice.

He hesitated, his gaze wrapping around hers and hinting at more than she'd ever believed possible from him. Lisa felt as if she'd stepped off a very high cliff. Then Brick's expression changed, and oozing discomfort, he looked away. "Yeah. Let's get it and go. It's almost time for us to meet the guy who's taking us snorkeling." He picked up one of the tablecloths. "Is it one size fits all or what?"

Fighting a ridiculous surge of disappointment and confusion, she forced her attention to the package. "No. It needs to fit the table." She glanced through the other packages on the table until she found the right size. "This one's right." She frowned and turned to Brick. "Are you sure?"

"I'm sure," he muttered, but he sounded irritated. "Let's go."

Lisa followed after him, trying to figure out what was going on inside his mind, inside his heart. During the cab ride to the ocean, she silently pondered his offer to contribute the tablecloth to her hope chest. Although she resisted attaching too much significance to it, she knew the gesture was completely at odds with his standoffish attitude toward marriage. She wanted to ask him about it, but she sensed a subtle, yet definite resistance within him.

By the time they reached the ocean, she gave up and pushed the issue to the back of her mind. Lisa could brood over Brick later while she was alone in her bed. Right now, she wanted to get a closer view of the Caribbean.

If Lisa found out, she was going to kill him, Brick thought as he watched her splendid rear end while she took another dive off the side of the boat. In approximately five minutes, the cruise ship was going bye-bye without them. He figured he could safely explain this in twenty years. He wasn't sure he would ever be able to confess that he'd sent those duds to her. Brick would rather face a dozen misfires than Lisa's wrath. And misfires were a blaster's nightmare.

With her absorption in exploring a coral reef, she'd completely lost track of the time. The afternoon had gone better than he'd hoped. She'd been at ease and so had he. As time wore on and Brick quietly shelled out more money to their guide, he'd decided that the setting was too perfect to waste.

He didn't want to take her back to the ship and the distractions it held. He also didn't enjoy deceiving her, and he hoped like hell all this game playing would be over soon.

She popped up out of the water, wearing a huge smile on her face. "Are you coming or not?"

Brick felt a tug deep in his gut. That smile could chase away every nightmare a man could have. Grabbing his snorkel and mask, he called back, "I'm coming." He jumped overboard into the clear, warm blue water and swam to her side. "You told me not to call you animal names, but if I didn't know better, I'd say you had gills."

Lisa laughed and playfully splashed him. "Stop!" Her eyes were bright with excitement. "There's so much to see."

"Yeah," he agreed around a lustful grin as he treaded water. "Like green eyes and dark eyelashes and a smile bright enough to blind a man." He dabbed a drop of water from the tip of her nose and curled his hands around her waist. "You look like some kind of sea goddess."

Lisa looked flattered, but skeptical. "What have you been drinking?"

Brick plastered a hurt expression on his face, but more than enjoyed the natural way she rested one of her hands on his shoulder. "You doubt my sincerity?"

Lisa turned serious. "I doubt a lot of things, but

never your sincerity." She took his hand. "C'mon. I want you to see this school of fish."

Wondering about those doubts of hers, Brick followed along. It was sheer delight to see how excited she got over each new sight.

She pulled him first this way, then that until their skin began to prune and Lisa finally realized they might have stayed too long at the fair.

She squinted her eyes at the sun. It wasn't quite as bright as it had been, she thought. It wasn't quite as warm either. She had no idea what time it was. She felt as if she'd barely been there an hour, but she had the sinking suspicion it had been far longer. A sliver of panic raced through her. "Brick." His face was in the water, so she nudged him to get his attention. "How long have we been out here?"

Brick shook the water from his hair and shrugged. "I left my watch on the boat."

He seemed incredibly calm, she noticed. "I think we'd better find out. The ship is supposed to leave at four and—"

"Hey, Johnny, what time is it?" Brick called to their guide.

The dark man held up four fingers on one hand and five on the other hand.

Lisa's heart sank. "Oh no! He must mean four-thirty. We've missed the cruise ship. What are we going to do? That's how we're supposed to get to Miami, and my flight home leaves tomorrow afternoon. Oh, I can't believe I did this. I feel so stupid, but snorkeling was such fun and—"

"Hold it. Hold it." Brick cut off her desperate monologue and pulled her toward the boat. "It's not as if we're destitute. Let's get back to the boat and figure out what to do. Johnny can probably help us out."

"I still can't believe I did this," she repeated for the next hour. Fighting a pang of guilt, she wondered if she'd subconsciously been trying to avoid returning to the ship. She was still shuddering from being called filly.

With Brick's reassurance and Johnny's hotel recommendation, Lisa's panic subsided. They arranged for their rooms, and while Brick booked flights for Miami for the following day, Lisa bought a sundress, underwear, and a few toiletries to tide her over.

When she finished her shower and changed, it was time for dinner. They ate lobster on the hotel restaurant veranda and watched the sun set over the Caribbean. It was a romantic setting, made even more romantic for Lisa because Brick was there to share it with her. Despite all her attempts to make herself feel differently, she couldn't change that. Something about the way he watched her, however, made her nervous.

He exuded a tension that had her wondering what was going on behind his violet eyes. She felt off center, as if something had changed, but she couldn't put her finger on what it was. She'd wondered if he would try to manipulate her into sharing his room, but he hadn't. Now she was dealing with a crazy mix of disappointment and relief. That was the problem with her when she was around Brick. He turned her priorities upside down, so that she didn't know whether she was coming or going, and when she was with him, she didn't really care. Sighing, she toyed with her dessert. "You've gotten quiet. Are you tired?"

He shook his head. "I've got something on my mind." He watched her for a moment, then lowered his voice. "Do you want to mutilate that pie some more, or would you like to take a walk on the beach?"

She immediately put down her fork and placed her napkin beside her plate. "Definitely the beach."

Within minutes, they were walking on the white sand. "This is wonderful," Lisa murmured, loving the feel of the breeze on her skin. "Do you think they could use a catering director down here?"

Brick slid his hand to her back. "Probably, but Chattanooga would miss you too much." He stopped and tilted her chin so that she would look at him. "I'd miss you too much."

Lisa's chest contracted. She took a shallow breath and shook her head. "You make it very hard for me to put you in the past and get on with my life," she whispered.

His gaze turned stormy. "I don't want you to put me in the past. I want to be in your future. I want—" He swore and turned away.

"Brick, what—?"

He sliced a hand through the air for her to wait.

She did, watching him curiously as he shoved his hands into his pockets and stared into the horizon. His white shirt billowed like a sail, contrasting with his tanned throat. Even though she felt confused and a little forlorn, his silhouette, strong and tender, affected her.

He was the man she would always want. The realization hit her so hard, it hurt. She would never love another. She wrapped her arms around herself as the chill of a second realization hit her. She might never marry and have the family she wanted either.

A terrible pain shot through her. She bit her lip against the burning sensation behind her eyes and wondered why it had to be this way.

Brick finally turned around, his gaze resolute yet uneasy. "I want you to marry me."

TWELVE

Speechless, Lisa stared at him in shock.

Brick's mouth was bone dry and his stomach was churning so much, he prayed he wouldn't lose his dinner. He took a few deep breaths, then reached for the antacids in his pocket. "You haven't said anything," he muttered in a raspy voice he hated.

Lisa blinked and shook her head. "You look as if you're going to throw up."

Brick scowled and popped a tablet into his mouth. "That's a helluva thing to say to a man who's just proposed to you."

Lisa bit her lip and moved closer to him. She squinted her eyes. "Brick, your face looks *green*."

"It is not!" Brick laced his fingers together and cracked his knuckles in frustration. "I don't care if I'm purple or polka-dotted. Do you want to marry me or not?"

A long silence followed where Lisa looked at him warily. She cleared her throat. "Well," she began, drawing out the word.

"Well what?" he asked through clenched teeth.

"Well . . . yes," she said, her voice full of doubt. "I guess," she added. "But you don't sound very happy about it."

Brick felt the tight, clenched feeling in his chest burst free. "Ah, Lisa." He pulled her into his arms. "I'm so damn happy, I don't think I can explain it." And he couldn't, he realized. Not yet. He'd felt the fear and done it anyway, but he wasn't ready to push himself further by explaining everything to her. Right now, she was in his arms and she'd said yes. Right now, he wanted to celebrate. He held her close and inhaled the scent of her hair. It was enough to make him feel high.

"Let's get some champagne and take it up to my room. Or your room." He speared his fingers through her hair and lifted her mouth to his for a kiss. She tasted of sensuality and sweetness and everything he'd always craved in his life. The way she curled into him sent his heart rate flying.

Finally dragging his mouth from hers, he tried to catch his breath. "I've always been better at showing than telling, Lisa. Let me show you how happy I am."

Looking dazed and fragile, Lisa closed her eyes. "I can't believe this is happening. Are you sure?"

She opened her eyes and her gaze searched his. "Are you really, really sure?"

Her fragility and uncertainty was so precious to him that he fully intended to rid her of all her doubts. "I'm really sure." And down underneath all his lifetime of fear, he was.

Brick lifted the glass of champagne. "To your eyes." He took a sip, placed it on the bedside table, then leaned forward and kissed her eyelids when she fluttered them closed. Lisa had sipped down a glass and a half of champagne and was deliciously dizzy.

"To your nose," he added, and kissed her nose.

Lisa rolled her eyes in disbelief. "My nose?"

"Are you questioning my sincerity?" he asked in a pseudostern voice.

"I—"

"To your mouth," he interrupted, and covered her mouth with his. Lisa sighed. Her niggling sense of uneasiness seemed to evaporate when his tongue dallied with hers. She gave herself over to the sensation of his mouth making love to hers. She gave herself over to the dream that had finally come true. She felt the gentle tug of his hands on her sundress and held her breath.

Brick pulled slightly away, his eyes heavy with sensuality. "I'm not finished with your mouth."

Lisa licked her lips, relishing his taste. "Good."

Brick groaned and pushed the dress from her body. His gaze traveled down her neck to linger on her breasts and trail a burning path down to her belly. Lisa felt a spinning sensation in her stomach.

As if he were working at keeping things slow, he lifted his gaze back to her face. "To your eyebrows," he said, and kissed them.

A giggle burst from her throat.

"You're not supposed to be laughing," he told her.

"Sorry," she said, but giggled again when he kissed her chin.

Brick gave a long-suffering sigh and lowered his mouth to nuzzle her throat. "To pot holders," he whispered.

Lisa's heart clutched, the desire to laugh quickly snuffed out.

He lowered his head still farther to the upper swell of her breasts. "To your aunt's afghan."

Honing in on her nipple, he drew it deeply into his mouth. Lisa felt the tug all the way to her womb.

He swirled his tongue around the sensitive peak, and she arched. "To rings and babies and Christmases together." He looked up at her, and Lisa knew this moment would be branded in her brain forever. Brick, his eyes full of love and desire, his hair mussed from her fingers, his shirt unbuttoned and pushed halfway down his arms. Promises and pleasure on his mouth. She lifted her hand to his jaw.

Brick closed his eyes and kissed her palm. "Always together."

Then he gently pushed her down on the bed and worked on showing instead of telling. Their clothes seemed to disappear, and then it was the brush of his skin against hers. The feeling of intimacy between them was a life force in itself.

Whispering love words into her ear, he touched her as if she were spun gold. And she could almost believe he thought she was. She smothered a gasp when he skimmed his mouth across her abdomen and down to her thigh. Her skin was sensitized to his every breath.

He stroked and kissed her breasts until she was beyond restless, and Lisa found she couldn't be only the receiver, she had to be the giver too. When she tried to nudge him onto his back, he protested.

"No," he muttered, his hands drawn to her like magnets. "I'm not finished. I want to—"

Lisa pressed an openmouthed kiss against his neck, and he broke off on a sigh. "I want to too," she said, rubbing her face into the soft hair of his hard chest.

Taking her turn to show tactile appreciation of

every inch of his body, Lisa stroked and caressed, drawing rough sounds of pleasure from his mouth. The pounding of his heart thrummed its way into her blood, making her lose all her inhibitions. Her lips followed her hands to the sensitive places of his body, behind his ear and down to his nipples. She kissed her way across his lower abdomen and gave a husky laugh when his stomach rippled.

She went from sensual amusement to serious, however, when she kissed his rigid arousal.

Brick swore and slipped his fingers through her hair. "Oh, Lord, Lisa . . ."

His arousal spurring hers, she took him into her mouth.

He swore again, a litany of desire and male need that she was desperate to fulfill.

"Lisa, stop!" he managed over a wild gasp, then let out a low animal-like groan when she slowly slid her mouth from him.

Her body liquid with readiness, Lisa stared up at him. His eyes glittered with passion, his mouth swollen from kisses, he turned her deliberately onto her back. Her uneven breaths matched his, his body was slick with perspiration as was hers. At her most basic and emotional level, she welcomed the purely male urge to mate she saw stamped on his features.

When she reached for him, he shook his head and drew her arms above her head, his fingers gently clasping her wrists. His hot gaze swept over her like a flash fire, and when he slid his fingers between her thighs, the delicious, slow building desire she felt burst out of control.

Struggling with the ache he seemed to make worse and better at the same time, she arched up from the bed. "Brick," she said with a gasp. "I need—" She moaned as he slid his finger inside her. "Oh, I want—" She arched again. "Brick, pleeeeease!"

"That's what I want to do, Lisa." He nudged her thighs apart and entered her inch by excruciating inch. Hissing through his teeth, he grimaced in pleasure. "That's what I want to do," he muttered, and stretched inside her. "Please."

He released her wrists and she immediately reached for him, pulling him as close as possible while his slow, steady thrusts took her farther from sanity with each stroke. As if from a distance, she heard herself call out his name while a spasm of exquisite pleasure shook her, pitching her up and over. And with an exultant cry of his own, Brick came tumbling after.

Brick and Lisa overslept the next morning and nearly missed their plane to Miami. The quick flight could have been a taxi ride considering how long it lasted. After making sure their luggage had been transferred by the cruise line, they settled in for the flight to Chattanooga.

Lisa laced her fingers through Brick's during takeoff.

He squeezed her hand. "Does flying bother you?"

She gave a wry smile. "Just takeoff and landing. I guess there's not much that can scare someone who works with explosives for a living."

Brick narrowed his eyes. "I wouldn't say that," he said in a dry, self-deprecating tone.

She looked at him curiously.

"I'll tell you about it some other time."

He didn't sound as if he were looking forward to it, she thought, but tried to shake off the uneasiness that made her nerve endings bristle. "Have you thought about when you want us to announce it?"

"Announce what?"

"Our engagement."

"Oh." Brick glanced away and shook his head. "I hadn't really thought about it. I figured we would decide all that later."

"Well, since we've got an hour-and-a-half flight ahead of us, there's no time like the present."

"Now?" he asked, consternation leaking through his tone while he took in her bright gaze.

Lisa hesitated, a furrow of confusion forming between her brows. "You don't want to discuss it?"

"No, no. It's fine," Brick rushed to reassure her, and shifted in his seat. His stomach began to burn. He released Lisa's hand and smoothed his own hand over his slacks. The prospect of an entire flight spent discussing wedding plans loomed before him. It was enough to make his palms sweat. He counted to twenty-five and took a deep breath.

Lisa pushed her hair behind her ear, then placed her hand on his arm. It was an affectionate gesture that warmed Brick's heart.

"There are a lot of things to decide, like where we want to live, when to get married, and how big a wedding we should have," she said. "But I guess we should decide if we want to tell people or wait a little while."

When she looked at him with such love in her eyes, he was ready to marry her on the spot. Maybe that was part of the solution to his problem, he thought, staying focused on her and how much she meant to him instead of the bad memories from his father's second marriage. Feeling a surge of devotion, he leaned closer and kissed her. "I don't want to wait. I think we've both waited long enough."

Visibly moved, Lisa gave a tremulous smile. "You have no idea how happy you've made me," she whispered.

Brick tried to hold on to that safe, yet glorious feeling for the rest of the flight, but sometimes the fear came back. Perhaps not as strong as it once was, but it still returned. It required a great deal of concentration for him to hide those moments from Lisa. He chewed his antacids and used some of the coping techniques. By the time the plane taxied up to the gate, he was relieved and exhausted.

Sensing that something wasn't quite right, Lisa felt her uneasiness climb. "Are you feeling okay?"

"Fine. I'm great," he said, crunching through another tablet.

Lisa frowned. The man she loved had finally proposed to her, but she couldn't tell if he felt trapped or happy. This wasn't a good sign, and she refused to push him into something he didn't want. Her chest felt achy at the thought that Brick might be doing this because *she* wanted it and he didn't. Pushing past her own unsteady emotions, she lowered her voice. "Brick, you don't sound completely sure about this. Do you regret proposing to me last night? If you do, then I'd rather you go ahead and say so now."

"I don't regret it. I absolutely don't regret it. It's just—" His glance slid away and he swore softly.

Lisa felt a sinking sensation in her stomach. She should have known it was too good to be true. The whole flight he'd been running hot and cold on her. "It's just what?" she said, feeling her stomach twist with dread.

He glanced around in frustration. "I can't talk about it now."

Disappointment and uncertainty hit her full force, delivering a knockout punch. After the beautiful night they'd shared together, she couldn't handle the flux of her own feelings, let alone his, anymore. Her heart splintered into fragments. Heedless of the fact that the crew hadn't given the passengers instructions for departing the airplane, she stood and scrambled past Brick.

"What are you doing?" He tried to grab her hand, but she shook it loose.

"I need to get out of here," she muttered desperately, hurrying down the aisle.

The attendant shot her a look of disapproval. "Miss, we haven't given passengers clearance. You—"

"I feel sick," Lisa managed over a swollen throat, and she wasn't lying. She was sick with a heart-crushing disappointment. Emotionally, she felt wounded and bleeding, and she needed to get away from everything and everyone, especially Brick. Hearing his footsteps behind her, she pleaded with the stewardess, "Please let me go."

The attendant immediately allowed her to exit, and Lisa ran through the terminal. Swiping at the tears that streamed down her face, she didn't care that people were staring. She didn't care that Brick was calling after her. She hoped she'd find a way to survive this debacle. Feeling like a fool was easy compared to dealing with her incredible pain and disillusionment.

Brick was alternately cursing the crowds and himself as he chased after Lisa. He should have gone ahead and told her everything the night before. Instead his ego had gotten in the way and he'd hoped he could keep it from her until he didn't feel so self-conscious about it. From a distance, he saw her squeeze through the door to the parking lot.

He darted around two elderly people and made it to the same door. Shoving it open, he scanned the parking lot. She was opening her car door. "Lisa," he shouted.

She gave him a desperate wild-eyed glance that shook him to the marrow of his bones, then she slid into her car and slammed the door.

Brick cursed, running across the taxi lane. A horn blared and tires screeched. Scooting onto the sidewalk, he kept his gaze fixed on Lisa's car. She backed out of her space onto the curb, missing the fire hydrant by an inch. He cringed.

She tore out of the parking lot, leaving a fair share of her tire tread on the pavement. Brick felt a kinship with that tire tread. He kicked the curb. This had gone on long enough. Lisa deserved to know what she was getting if she dared to take him back. A heavy dread dragging at his gut, he headed for his own car. They would have to get their luggage later.

Within ten minutes, he pulled into her apartment parking lot and was knocking on her door for all he was worth. "Lisa, open up. We've gotta talk."

When there was no answer, Brick just kept on. "I've got something I've got to explain to you." He noticed a few people stopping and looking at him curiously. "If I have to spill my guts in front of your neighbors," he called, full of determination, "I'll do it."

When she still didn't answer, he took a deep breath. "If you're wondering why I get tense every time we talk about marriage, it's because I've got something called gamophobia. Dr. Michaels doesn't call it that, but—"

The door whipped open, and Lisa stood there with a box of tissues in her hand and a shocked expression on her face. "Gamowhat?"

Brick met her gaze. "Are you sure you want to hear this? It's not pretty, but it's real." His heart was pounding a mile a minute. "And it's the truth."

He felt disgust for hurting her when he saw how her eyes were still shadowed with pain. She hesitated for what seemed like a lifetime, and Brick fully expected her to slam the door in his face. "I want to hear," she finally said in a low voice, and backed away from the door.

Following her to her den, Brick looked inside himself for the strength to get through the next few minutes. "You might want to sit down. This is gonna take a while."

Lisa sat stiffly in a chair and blew her nose. "Go ahead."

Brick crammed his fists into his pockets. "This is for damn sure the hardest thing I've ever done. I don't even know where to start."

Lisa chewed on her upper lip. "What's gamophobia?"

"Fear of marriage." He spit out the words like grenades.

Complete silence followed his answer.

She shook her head as if she were unable to comprehend the definition.

Brick held up a hand and sighed. "Just listen. You might not want to have anything to do with me when I finish, but for now, try to listen."

She tentatively nodded, and Brick turned toward the window, staring unseeingly, as he began his explanation. "I already told you about how my mother died and my father remarried this—" He groped for something kind. "Witch," he said generously. "He might as well have died when my mother did, and he shouldn't have married Eunice. I guess he thought he was doing it for us." Brick shrugged.

"Anyway, it happened at a bad time for me. I was twelve, and it scared the spit out of me to see what happened to my dad. I was just a kid and I felt helpless. Dr. Michaels said—"

"Dr. Michaels?" Lisa interrupted, clearly struggling to keep up with his explanation.

He looked over his shoulder at her. "Dr. Michaels is the counselor I went to see after that night you and I spent at the hotel."

She looked taken aback. "I had no idea."

Feeling a faint bit of encouragement that she hadn't thrown him out yet, he turned the rest of the way to face her. "Dr. Michaels said since I haven't talked all this out with someone else, it has stayed with me."

"Is this why you eat antacids like candy whenever we talk about marriage?"

Brick felt uncomfortable, but he nodded. "My stomach turns, my palms sweat, my heart races."

Lisa balled up the tissue. "Then why on earth did you ask me to marry you?"

Brick felt his heart twist. "Because I love you, and I want to be with you forever."

She snatched another tissue from the box. He saw her lip quiver and wanted to hold her so bad, he ached. She pressed the tissue to the corner of her eye, then looked at him. "You're not making any sense," she said in a voice that was little more than a whisper.

"I know," Brick agreed, and knelt beside her chair. He suffered a little more when she looked away from him. "And I'm probably gonna be dealing with this for a while longer. You don't get over half a lifetime of irrational fear in a few easy sessions. It's damn hard work. I wouldn't have even admitted that I had a real problem if it hadn't been for you. And if I hadn't felt like my guts had been torn out, I wouldn't have decided to call a counselor. It was one of the toughest things I've ever done to admit that I might need help. That I couldn't take care of my problem by myself." He hesitated. "Dr. Michaels suggested that I ask you to come with me."

Lisa's gaze swerved to meet his.

"But I couldn't do it," he admitted. "You didn't want to see me anymore, and what if this was something I never got over? It's not as if I'm any prize." He ran his hand through his hair. "By the time I went on the cruise, I started thinking I would get past this, but you were furious with me."

Lisa's eyes filled with tears and she tentatively covered his hand with hers. "I always thought you were a prize. Oh, Brick, I wish you had told me. I wish you hadn't had to go through this by yourself. I wish—" She broke off and gulped.

Brick closed his hand around hers. He shut his eyes for a quick second against the clench deep in his soul. Hers was the sweetest touch he'd ever experienced. He craved it whether he was feeling great or lousy. He sucked in a deep breath and looked straight into her eyes. "I want to marry you. My hands might sweat. I might have to chew a truckload of antacids, but I want you, Lisa."

She shook her head in confusion. "But if the thought of marriage bothers you that much—"

He shook his head. "No. I worked with Dr. Michaels to come up with a different view of marriage—full of love. He says it might take a while, but my physical responses will eventually go away. Even now, every time I start to feel that horrible fear, I tell myself how good it's gonna be when you and I are together for always."

"Do you really believe that?"

"I do," he said as if he were making a vow. "But the question for you is now that you know all the dirt on me, do you still want me?"

Lisa would almost swear he was holding his breath for her response. "Are you kidding?" she asked.

His face fell as if she'd slapped him, and she knew immediately that he'd misunderstood her. Her voice volume cranked up, despite her efforts to keep it lowered. "I can't believe you'd even ask me that, Brick Pendleton. When have I not wanted you?" She stood and urged him to his feet. "I tried to forget you, ignore you, not want you, not need you, not love you. And I failed completely on all counts." Her voice was husky with emotion. She put her hands on his shirt and pulled him closer. "I wish you'd told me about this, so I could have been there for you."

Brick looked as if she'd given him back his life when he thought it had been taken away. "In a way, I think you always were. I had to get to the point that I was hurting like hell before I faced it." He gave a rough sigh and put his hand over hers. "I had to have a real good reason to change. And that reason was you."

Her heart swelled with love. Lisa had never admired him more. This big, powerful man had found the courage to fight his demons and he'd won. Many men wouldn't even have attempted it. She was awed by his strength and resilience. Tears filled her eyes and she shook her head helplessly. "I don't know what to say. I'm in awe of you."

Brick's jaw tightened with emotion. "I wondered if you'd think less of me."

"Never," she said emphatically. God knew, she wanted to make this clear as glass. "How could I? You walked into your lions' den and came out whole. Very few would be willing to do that." Fresh tears streamed down her cheeks. "And to think—" Her voice was squeezed out by the lump in her throat. She swallowed hard. "To think that you did it because you love me?"

Muttering her name, Brick pulled her tightly

against him, and Lisa pressed her face into his chest, soaking up his closeness. She felt his strength, his vulnerability, and his love in a way she never had before.

"I'm gonna ask this one last time," he said in a hoarse voice. "You better think long and hard, because once you give your answer, that's it. No second thoughts, no stalling, no backing out. You're stuck." He nudged her head up to meet his compelling, possessive gaze. "Will you marry me?"

"Try and stop me," she said, and met him halfway for a kiss.

EPILOGUE

Six months later, Brick was a free man.

He'd thrown away his last pack of antacid tablets months earlier. His palms were dry. His heart rate was slightly elevated, but that was due to excitement, not fear. Although he wore a tux with tails, he could have posed for a deodorant commercial. His predominant emotion as he stood with his brothers and the minister at the front of the church was eagerness.

Troy had told a few worn Elvis jokes in an obvious attempt to either rattle Brick or put him at ease. Before the ceremony each of his brothers had asked him if he was doing okay. Brick grinned to himself. If he'd been the least bit nervous, all that asking would have irritated him. Instead it warmed him to hear their concern. He winked at Carly, who was one of Lisa's bridesmaids.

The organ music swelled and so did his heart, because at that moment there stood his bride at the back of the church. Lisa's bright green gaze met his as she made her way down the aisle with her daddy beside her. She smiled. Brick felt his grin grow until he was sure it took up his whole face. Lord, love felt good. He was thankful he hadn't missed it, hadn't missed her.

It was a moment that would stay frozen in his mind until the end of time—the vision of Lisa in her white dress and veil with eyes that told how much she loved him every step of the way.

When they reached the front, her father kissed her cheek then joined Lisa's hand with Brick's. Brick brought her hand to his lips.

"Dearly beloved," the minister said, and Brick knew beyond the shadow of a doubt that he had found the dearly beloved woman who would last him a lifetime.

Later that night, Brick lay on the bed, his body still humming with satisfaction. His head was reeling, his breath was uneven. He stared at his new wife as she cuddled against his side. "What possessed you to do a strip tease on tonight of all nights?"

Her eyes closed, Lisa smiled. It was a sultry,

woman's smile full of knowledge. "You said it was your fantasy."

"Yeah, but—"

"I thought it was only fair. You've taken care of all of my fantasies." She rubbed her cheek against his shoulder and opened her eyes. "Are you complaining?"

"Hell, no." He gave her a thorough kiss to prove it.

Lisa sighed when he slowly pulled his lips away from hers. "You know how much I admire you, adore you, and love you, but now that we're married, I guess I can make a confession."

More curious than tense, he turned his head so he could see her face. "Yeah?"

Her gaze was frankly appreciative. "There's something incredibly sexy about a man who's walked through fire and come out better."

His chest swelled with pride. The fact that she knew him inside out and would say something like that made him feel ten feet tall. He pulled her warm, responsive body on top of his and felt the beginning surge of arousal. "Is that so?"

Her eyes lit with humor. "It is."

"Then maybe I'd better tell you another one of my fantasies," he said in a big-bad-bear voice and caught her laughter in his mouth with a kiss that set the night to music all over again.

Over the next months Brick found the adjustment to married life more enjoyable than he'd ever dreamed. And he didn't reach for another antacid tablet until Lisa's ultrasound showed three babies instead of one.

THE EDITOR'S CORNER

Since the inception of LOVESWEPT in 1983, we've been known as the most innovative publisher of category romance. We were the first to publish authors under their real names and show their photographs in the books. We originated interconnected "series" books and established theme months. And now, after publishing over 700 books, we are once again changing the face of category romance.

Starting next month, we are introducing a brand-new LOVESWEPT look. We're sure you'll agree with us that it's distinctive and outstanding—nothing less than the perfect showcase for your favorite authors and the wonderful stories they write.

A second change is that we are now publishing four LOVESWEPTs a month instead of six. With so many romances on the market today, we want to provide you with only the very best in romantic fiction. We know that you want quality, not quantity, and we are as committed as ever to giving you love stories you'll never forget, by authors you'll always remember. We are especially proud to debut our new look with four sizzling romances from four of our most talented authors.

Starting off our new look is Mary Kay McComas with **WAIT FOR ME**, LOVESWEPT #702. Oliver Carey saves Holly Loftin's life during an earthquake with a split-second tackle, but only when their eyes meet does he feel the earth tremble and her compassionate soul reach out to his. He is intrigued by her need to help others, enchanted by her appetite for simple pleasures, but now he has to show her that their differences can be their strengths and that, more than anything, they belong together. Mary Kay will have you laughing and crying with this touching romance.

The ever-popular Kay Hooper is back with her unique blend of romantic mystery and spicy wit in **THE HAUNTING OF JOSIE**, LOVESWEPT #703. Josie Douglas decides that Marc Westbrook, her gorgeous landlord, would have made a good warlock, with his raven-dark hair, silver eyes, and even a black cat in his arms! She chose the isolated house as a refuge, a place to put the past to rest, but now Marc insists on fighting her demons . . . and why does he so resemble the ghostly figure who beckons to her from the head of the stairs? Kay once more demonstrates her talent for seduction and suspense in this wonderful romance.

Theresa Gladden proves that opposites attract in **PERFECT TIMING**, LOVESWEPT #704. Jenny Johnson isn't looking for a new husband, no matter how many hunks her sister sends her way, but Carter Dalton's cobalt-blue eyes mesmerize her into letting his daughter join her girls' club—and inviting him to dinner! The free-spirited rebel is all wrong for him: messy house, too many pets, wildly disorganized—but he can't resist a woman who promises to fill the empty spaces he didn't know he had. Theresa's spectacular romance will leave you breathless.

Last but certainly not least is **TAMING THE PIRATE**, LOVESWEPT #705, from the supertalented Ruth Owen. When investigator Gabe Ramirez sees Laurie Palmer, she stirs to life the appetites of his buccaneer ancestors and makes him long for the golden lure of her smile. She longs to trade her secrets for one kiss from his brigand's lips, but once he knows why she is on the run, will he betray the woman he's vowed will never escape his arms? You won't forget this wonderful story from Ruth.

Happy reading,

With warmest wishes,

Nita Taublib

Nita Taublib
Deputy Publisher

P.S. Don't miss the exciting women's novels from Bantam that are coming your way in August—**MIDNIGHT WARRIOR**, by *New York Times* bestselling author Iris Johansen, is a spellbinding tale of pursuit, possession, and passion that extends from the wilds of Normandy to untamed medieval England; **BLUE MOON** is a powerful and romantic novel of love and families by the exceptionally talented Luanne Rice. *The New York Times Book Review* calls it "a rare combination of realism and romance"; **VELVET**, by Jane Feather, is a spectacular novel of danger and deception in which a beautiful woman risks all for revenge and love; **THE WITCH DANCE**, by Peggy Webb, is a poignant story of two lovers whose passion breaks every rule. We'll be giving you a sneak peek at these terrific books in next month's LOVESWEPTs. And immediately following this page, look for a preview of the exciting romances from Bantam that are *available now!*

Don't miss these extraordinary books by
your favorite Bantam authors

On sale in June:

MISTRESS
by *Amanda Quick*

WILDEST DREAMS
by *Rosanne Bittner*

DANGEROUS TO LOVE
by *Elizabeth Thornton*

AMAZON LILY
by *Theresa Weir*

MISTRESS

Available in hardcover
by the *New York Times*
bestselling author

AMANDA QUICK

With stories rife with wicked humor, daring intrigue, and heart-stopping passion, Amanda Quick has become a writer unmatched in the field of romantic fiction. Now the author of fourteen New York Times bestselling novels offers another unforgettable tale as a proper spinster embarks on a delicious masquerade and a handsome earl finds himself tangling with the most exotic and captivating mistress London has ever known.

"Power, passion, tragedy, and triumph
are Rosanne Bittner's hallmarks. Again and
again, she brings readers to tears."
—*Romantic Times*

WILDEST DREAMS
by

ROSANNE
BITTNER

Against the glorious panorama of big sky country, award-winning Rosanne Bittner creates a sweeping saga of passion, excitement, and danger ... as a beautiful young woman and a rugged ex-soldier struggle against all odds to carve out an empire—and to forge a magnificent love.

Here is a look at this powerful novel ...

Lettie walked ahead of him into the shack, swallowing back an urge to retch. She gazed around the cabin, noticed a few cracks between the boards that were sure to let in cold drafts in the winter. A rat scurried across the floor, and she stepped back. The room was very small, perhaps fifteen feet square, with a potbellied stove in one corner, a few shelves built against one wall, and a crudely built table in the middle of the room, with two crates to serve as chairs. The bed was made from pine, with ropes for springs and no mattress on top. She was glad her mother had given her two feather mattresses before they parted. Never had she longed more fervently to be with her family back at the spacious home they had left behind in St.

Joseph, where people lived in reasonable numbers, and anything they needed was close at hand.

Silently, she untied and removed the wool hat she'd been wearing. She was shaken by her sense of doubt, not only over her choice to come to this lonely, desolate place, but also over her decision to marry. She loved Luke, and he had been attentive and caring and protective throughout their dangerous, trying journey to get here; but being his wife meant fulfilling other needs he had not yet demanded of her. This was the very first time they had been truly alone since marrying at Fort Laramie. When Luke had slept in the wagon with her, he had only held her. Was he waiting for her to make the first move; or had he patiently been waiting for this moment, when he had her alone? Between the realization that he would surely expect to consummate their marriage now, and the knowledge that she would spend the rest of the winter holed up in this tiny cabin, with rats running over her feet, she felt panic building.

"Lettie?"

She was startled by the touch of Luke's hand on her shoulder. She gasped and turned to look up at him, her eyes wide with fear and apprehension. "I . . . I don't know if I can stay here, Luke." Oh, why had she said that? She could see the hurt in his eyes. He should be angry. Maybe he would throw her down and have his way with her now, order her to submit to her husband, yell at her for being weak and selfish, tell her she would stay here whether she liked it or not.

He turned, looked around the tiny room, looked back at her with a smile of resignation on his face. "I can't blame you there. I don't know why I even considered this. I guess in all my excitement . . ." He sighed deeply. "I'll take you back to Billings in the morning. It's not much of a town, but maybe I can find a safe place for you and Nathan to stay while I make things more livable around here."

"But . . . you'd be out here all alone."

He shrugged, walking over to the stove and opening the door. "I knew before I ever came here there would be a lot of lonely living I'd have to put up with." He picked up some kindling from a small pile that lay near the stove and stacked it inside. "When you have a dream, you simply do what you have to do to realize it." He turned to face her. "I told you it won't be like this forever, Lettie, and it won't."

His eyes moved over her, and she knew what he wanted. He simply loved and respected her too much to ask for it. A wave of guilt rushed through her, and she felt like crying. "I'm sorry, Luke. I've disappointed you in so many ways already."

He frowned, coming closer. "I never said that. I don't blame you for not wanting to stay here. I'll take you back to town and you can come back here in the spring." He placed his hands on her shoulders. "I love you, Lettie. I never want you to be unhappy or wish you had never married me. I made you some promises, and I intend to keep them."

A lump seemed to rise in her throat. "You'd really take me to Billings? You wouldn't be angry about it?"

Luke studied her face. He wanted her so, but was not sure how to approach the situation because of what she had been through. He knew there was a part of her that wanted him that way, but he had not seen it in her eyes since leaving Fort Laramie. He had only seen doubt and fear. "I told you I'd take you. I wouldn't be angry."

She suddenly smiled, although there were tears in her eyes. "That's all I need to know. I . . . I thought you took it for granted, just because I was your wife . . . that you'd demand . . ."

She threw her arms around him, resting her face against his thick fur jacket. "Oh, Luke, forgive me. You don't have to take me back. As long as I know I *can* go back, that's all I need to know. Does that make any sense?"

He grinned. "I think so."

Somewhere in the distance they heard the cry of a bobcat. Combined with the groaning mountain wind, the sounds only accentuated how alone they really were, a good five miles from the only town, and no sign of civilization for hundreds of miles beyond that. "I can't let you stay out here alone. You're my husband. I belong here with you," Lettie said, still clinging to him.

Luke kissed her hair, her cheek. She found herself turning to meet his lips, and he explored her mouth savagely then. She felt lost in his powerful hold, buried in the fur jacket, suddenly weak. How well he fit this land, so tall and strong and rugged and determined. She loved him all the more for it.

He left her mouth, kissed her neck. "I'd better get a fire going, bring in—"

"Luke." She felt her heart racing as all her fears began to melt away. She didn't know how to tell him, what to do. She could only look into those handsome blue eyes and say his name. She met his lips again, astonished at the sudden hunger in her soul. How could she have considered letting this poor man stay out here alone, when he had a wife and child who could help him, love him? And how could she keep denying him the one thing he had every right to take for himself? Most of all, how could she deny her own sudden desires, this surprising awakening of woman that ached to be set free?

"Luke," she whispered. "I want to be your wife, Luke, in every way. I want to be one with you and know that it's all right. I don't want to be afraid any more."

DANGEROUS TO LOVE
by Elizabeth Thornton

"A major, major talent . . . a genre superstar."
—*Rave Reviews*

Dangerous. Wild. Reckless. Those were the words that passed through Serena Ward's mind the moment Julian Raynor entered the gaming hall. If anyone could penetrate Serena's disguise—and jeopardize the political fugitives she was delivering to freedom—surely it would be London's most notorious gamester. Yet when the militia storms the establishment in search of traitors, Raynor provides just the pretext Serena needs to escape. But Serena is playing with fire . . . and before the night is through she will find herself surrendering to the heat of unsuspected desires.

The following is a sneak preview of what transpires that evening in a private room above the gaming hall. . .

"Let's start over, shall we?" said Julian. He returned to the chair he had vacated. "And this time, I shall try to keep myself well in check. No, don't move. I rather like you kneeling at my feet in an attitude of submission."

He raised his wine glass and imbibed slowly. "Now you," he said. When she made to take it from him, he shook his head. "No, I shall hold it. Come closer."

Once again she found herself between his thighs. She didn't know what to do with her hands, but he knew.

"Place them on my thighs," he said, and Serena obeyed. Beneath her fingers, she could feel the hard masculine muscles bunch and strain. She was also acutely aware of the movements of the militia as they combed the building for Jacobites.

"Drink," he said, holding the rim of the glass to her lips, tipping it slightly.

Wine flooded her mouth and spilled over. Choking, she swallowed it.

"Allow me," he murmured. As one hand cupped her neck, his head descended and his tongue plunged into her mouth.

Shock held her rigid as his tongue thrust, and thrust again, circling, licking at the dregs of wine in her mouth, lapping it up with avid enjoyment. When she began to struggle, his powerful thighs tightened against her, holding her effortlessly. Her hands went to his chest to push him away, and slipped between the parted edges of his shirt. Warm masculine flesh quivered beneath the pads of her fingertips. Splaying her hands wide, with every ounce of strength, she shoved at him, trying to free herself.

He released her so abruptly that she tumbled to the floor. Scrambling away from him, she came up on her knees. They were both breathing heavily.

Frowning, he rose to his feet and came to tower over her. "What game are you playing now?"

"No game," she quickly got out. "You are going too fast for me." She carefully rose to her feet and began to inch away from him. "We have yet to settle on my . . . my remuneration."

"Remuneration?" He laughed softly. "Sweetheart, I have already made up my mind that for a woman of your unquestionable talents, no price is too high."

These were not the words that Serena wanted to hear, nor did she believe him. Men did not like greedy women. Although she wasn't supposed to know it, long before his marriage, her brother, Jeremy, had given his mistress her *congé* because the girl was too demanding. What was it the girl had wanted?

Her back came up against the door to the bedchamber. One hand curved around the door-knob in a reflexive movement, the other clutched the door-jamb for support.

Licking her lips, she said, "I . . . I shall want my own house."

He cocked his head to one side. As though musing to himself, he said, "I've never had a woman in my keeping. Do you know, for the first time, I can see the merit in it? Fine, you shall have your house."

He took a step closer, and she flattened herself against the door. "And . . . and my own carriage?" She could hardly breathe with him standing so close to her.

"Done." His eyes were glittering.

When he lunged for her, she cried out and flung herself into the bed-chamber, slamming the door quickly, bracing her shoulder against it as her fingers fumbled for the key.

One kick sent both door and Serena hurtling back. He stood framed in the doorway, the light behind him, and every sensible thought went out of her head. Dangerous. Reckless. Wild. This was all a game to him!

He feinted to the left, and she made a dash for the door, twisting away as his hands reached for her. His fingers caught on the back of her gown, ripping it to the waist. One hand curved around her arm, sending her sprawling against the bed.

There was no candle in the bed-chamber, but the lights from the tavern's courtyard filtered through the window casting a luminous glow. He was shedding the last of his clothes. Although everything in her revolted against it, she knew that the time had come to reveal her name.

Summoning the remnants of her dignity, she said, "You should know that I am no common doxy. I am a high-born lady."

He laughed in that way of his that she was coming to thoroughly detest. "I know," he said, "and I am to play the conqueror. Sweetheart, those games are all very well in their place. But the time for games is over. I want a real woman in my arms tonight, a willing one and not some character from a fantasy."

She turned his words over in her mind and

could make no sense of them. Seriously doubting the man's sanity, she cried out, "Touch me and you will regret it to your dying day. Don't you understand anything? I am a lady. I . . ."

He fell on her and rolled with her on the bed. Subduing her easily with the press of his body, he rose above her. "Have done with your games. I am Julian. You are Victoria. I am your protector. You are my mistress. Yield to me, sweeting."

Bought and paid for—that was what was in his mind. She was aware of something else. He didn't want to hurt or humiliate her. He wanted to have his way with her. He thought he had that right.

He wasn't moving, or forcing his caresses on her. He was simply holding her, watching her with an unfathomable expression. "Julian," she whispered, giving him his name in an attempt to soften him. "Victoria Noble is not my real name."

"I didn't think it was," he said, and kissed her.

His mouth was gentle; his tongue caressing, slipping between her teeth, not deeply, not threateningly, but inviting her to participate in the kiss. For a moment, curiosity held her spellbound. She had never been kissed like this before. It was like sinking into a bath of spiced wine. It was sweet and intoxicating, just like the taste of him.

Shivering, she pulled out of the embrace and stared up at him. His brows were raised, questioning her. All she need do was tell him her name and he would let her go.

Suddenly it was the last thing she wanted to do.

AMAZON LILY

by the spectacular

Theresa Weir

"You must be the Lily-Libber who's going to San Reys."

The deep voice that came slicing through Corey's sleep-fogged brain was gravelly and rough-edged.

She dragged open heavy-lidded eyes to find herself contemplating a ragged pair of grubby blue tennis shoes. She allowed her gaze to pan slowly northward, leaving freeze-framed images etched in her mind's eye: long jeans faded to almost white except along the stitching; a copper waistband button with moldy lettering; a large expanse of chest-filled, sweat-soaked T-shirt; a stubbly field of several days growth of whiskers; dark aviator sunglasses that met the dusty, sweaty brim of a New York Yankees baseball cap.

Corey's head was bent back at an uncomfortable angle. Of course, Santarém, Brazil, wasn't Illinois, and this person certainly wasn't like any case she'd ever handled in her job as a social worker.

The squalid air-taxi building was really little more than a shed, and it had been crowded before, with just Corey and the files. But now, with this man in front of her giving off his angry aura . . . She couldn't see his eyes, but she could read enough of his expression to know that she was being regarded as a lower form of life or something he might have scraped off the bottom off his shoe.

She knew she wasn't an American beauty. Her skin was too pale, her brown eyes too large for her small face, giving her a fragile, old-world appearance that was a burden in these modern times. People had a tendency to either overlook her completely or coddle her. But his reaction was something totally new.

The man's attention shifted from her to the smashed red packet in his hand. He pulled out a flattened nonfilter cigarette, smoothed it until it was somewhat round, then stuck it in the corner of his mouth. One hand moved across the front of the faded green T-shirt that clung damply to his corded muscles. He slapped at the breast pocket. Not finding what he was searching for, both of his hands moved to the front pockets of the ancient jeans that covered those long, athletic legs. There was a frayed white horizontal rip across his right knee, tan skin and sun-bleached hair showing through. Change jingled as he rummaged around to finally pull out a damp, wadded-up book of matches.

"Damn," he muttered after the third match failed to light. "Gotta quit sweating so much." He tossed the bedraggled matchbook to the floor. Cigarette still in his mouth, his hands began a repeat search of his pockets.

Corey reached over to where her twill shoulder bag was lying on a stack of tattered *Mad* magazines. She unzipped a side pocket and pulled out the glossy black and gold matches she'd been saving to add to her matchbook collection.

He grabbed them without so much as a thank-you. "That's right—" he said, striking a match, "you girl scouts are always prepared." He shook out the match and tossed it to the floor.

"Are you Mike Jones?" She hoped to God he wasn't the pilot she was waiting for.

"No." He inhaled deeply, then exhaled, blowing a thick cloud of smoke her direction.

"Do you know when Mr. Jones will be here?" she asked, willing her eyes not to bat against the smoke.

"*Mister* Jones had a slight setback. He was unconscious last time I saw him." The man read the ornate advertisement for the Black Tie restaurant on the match cover, then tucked the matches into the breast pocket of his T-shirt. The knuckles of his hand were red and swollen, one finger joint cracked and covered with dried blood.

"I found Jones in a local cantina, drunk out of his mind and just itching to fly. Had a little trouble convincing him it would be in his best interest if he stayed on the ground. My name's Ash—Asher Adams, and it looks like I'll be flying you to the reserve. If you still want to go."

Corey pushed her earlier thoughts to the back of her mind. "Of course I still want to go." She hadn't come this far to back out now.

"You want my advice?" He pulled off the navy-blue cap and swiped at his sweating forehead before slapping the cap back over shaggy brown hair. "Go back home. Get married. Have babies. Why is it you women have to prove you're men? You come here thrill-seeking so you can go home and be some kind of small-town hero. So your whole puny story can be printed up in a little four-page county paper and you can travel around to all the local clubs and organizations with your slide presentation, and all your friends can ooh and aah over you."

Corey felt heated anger flushing her face. She pressed her lips together in a firm, stubborn line.

What an obnoxious boor! In her years as a social worker, she'd never, *never* come across anyone like him. And thank God for that, she fumed.

Asher Adams took another drag off his cigarette, then flopped down in the chair across from her, legs sticking out in front of him, crossed at the ankles. "Go back home," he said in a weary voice. "This is real. It isn't some Humphrey Bogart movie. This isn't Sleepyville, Iowa, or wherever the hell you're from—"

"Pleasant Grove, Illinois," she flatly informed him. "And I don't need your advice. I don't want it." Who did this overbearing man think he was? She hadn't taken vacation time to come here and be insulted by an ill-tempered woman-hater. And he talked as if she planned to settle in the jungles of Brazil. There was nothing further from her mind.

She zipped her bag and grabbed up her cream-colored wool jacket. "I'd like to leave now."

And don't miss these fabulous romances
from Bantam Books, on sale in July:

MIDNIGHT WARRIOR
by the *New York Times* bestselling author
Iris Johansen
"Iris Johansen is a master among
master stoytellers."
—*Affaire de Coeur*

BLUE MOON
by the nationally bestselling author
Luanne Rice
"Luanne Rice proves herself a
nimble virtuoso."
—*The Washington Post Book World*

VELVET
by the highly acclaimed
Jane Feather
"An author to treasure."
—*Romantic Times*

THE WITCH DANCE
by the incomparable
Peggy Webb
"Ms. Webb has an inventive mind
brimming with originality that makes
all of her books special reading."
—*Romantic Times*

OFFICIAL RULES

To enter the sweepstakes below carefully follow all instructions found elsewhere in this offer.

The **Winners Classic** will award prizes with the following approximate maximum values: 1 Grand Prize: $26,500 (or $25,000 cash alternate); 1 First Prize: $3,000; 5 Second Prizes: $400 each; 35 Third Prizes: $100 each; 1,000 Fourth Prizes: $7.50 each. Total maximum retail value of Winners Classic Sweepstakes is $42,500. Some presentations of this sweepstakes may contain individual entry numbers corresponding to one or more of the aforementioned prize levels. To determine the Winners, individual entry numbers will first be compared with the winning numbers preselected by computer. For winning numbers not returned, prizes will be awarded in random drawings from among all eligible entries received. Prize choices may be offered at various levels. If a winner chooses an automobile prize, all license and registration fees, taxes, destination charges and, other expenses not offered herein are the responsibility of the winner. If a winner chooses a trip, travel must be complete within one year from the time the prize is awarded. Minors must be accompanied by an adult. Travel companion(s) must also sign release of liability. Trips are subject to space and departure availability. Certain black-out dates may apply.

The following applies to the sweepstakes named above:

No purchase necessary. You can also enter the sweepstakes by sending your name and address to: P.O. Box 508, Gibbstown, N.J. 08027. Mail each entry separately. Sweepstakes begins 6/1/93. Entries must be received by 12/30/94. Not responsible for lost, late, damaged, misdirected, illegible or postage due mail. Mechanically reproduced entries are not eligible. All entries become property of the sponsor and will not be returned.

Prize Selection/Validations: Selection of winners will be conducted no later than 5:00 PM on January 28, 1995, by an independent judging organization whose decisions are final. Random drawings will be held at 1211 Avenue of the Americas, New York, N.Y. 10036. Entrants need not be present to win. Odds of winning are determined by total number of entries received. Circulation of this sweepstakes is estimated not to exceed 200 million. All prizes are guaranteed to be awarded and delivered to winners. Winners will be notified by mail and may be required to complete an affidavit of eligibility and release of liability which must be returned within 14 days of date on notification or alternate winners will be selected in a random drawing. Any prize notification letter or any prize returned to a participating sponsor, Bantam Doubleday Dell Publishing Group, Inc., its participating divisions or subsidiaries, or the independent judging organization as undeliverable will be awarded to an alternate winner. Prizes are not transferable. No substitution for prizes except as offered or as may be necessary due to unavailability, in which case a prize of equal or greater value will be awarded. Prizes will be awarded approximately 90 days after the drawing. All taxes are the sole responsibility of the winners. Entry constitutes permission (except where prohibited by law) to use winners' names, hometowns, and likenesses for publicity purposes without further or other compensation. Prizes won by minors will be awarded in the name of parent or legal guardian.

Participation: Sweepstakes open to residents of the United States and Canada, except for the province of Quebec. Sweepstakes sponsored by Bantam Doubleday Dell Publishing Group, Inc., (BDD), 1540 Broadway, New York, NY 10036. Versions of this sweepstakes with different graphics and prize choices will be offered in conjunction with various solicitations or promotions by different subsidiaries and divisions of BDD. Where applicable, winners will have their choice of any prize offered at level won. Employees of BDD, its divisions, subsidiaries, advertising agencies, independent judging organization, and their immediate family members are not eligible.

Canadian residents, in order to win, must first correctly answer a time limited arithmetical skill testing question. Void in Puerto Rico, Quebec and wherever prohibited or restricted by law. Subject to all federal, state, local and provincial laws and regulations. For a list of major prize winners (available after 1/29/95): send a self-addressed, stamped envelope entirely separate from your entry to: Sweepstakes Winners, P.O. Box 517, Gibbstown, NJ 08027. Requests must be received by 12/30/94. DO NOT SEND ANY OTHER CORRESPONDENCE TO THIS P.O. BOX.

Don't miss these fabulous
Bantam women's fiction titles

On Sale in July

MIDNIGHT WARRIOR
by Iris Johansen
New York Times bestselling author of *The Beloved Scoundrel*
A passionate new tale of danger, adventure, and romance
that sweeps from a Saxon stronghold to a lovers' bower in
the cool, jade green forests of Wales.
❏ *29946-8 $5.99/6.99 in Canada*

BLUE MOON
by Luanne Rice
The moving novel of a family that discovers the everyday
magic of life and the extraordinary power of love.
"Eloquent...A moving and complete tale of the complicated
phenomenon we call family."—*People*
❏ *56818-3 $5.99/6.99 in Canada*

VELVET
by Jane Feather, bestselling, award-winning author of *Vixen*
"An author to treasure.."—*Romantic Times*
❏ *56469-2 $5.50/6.99 in Canada*

WITCH DANCE
by Peggy Webb
"Ms. Webb exquisitely plays on all our heartstrings."
—*Romantic Times*
❏ *56057-3 $4.99/5.99 in Canada*

Ask for these books at your local bookstore
or use this page to order.

❏ Please send me the books I have checked above. I am enclosing $ _____ (add $2.50
to cover postage and handling). Send check or money order, no cash or C. O. D.'s please.

Name _____

Address _____

City/ State/ Zip _____

Send order to: Bantam Books, Dept. FN143, 2451 S. Wolf Rd., Des Plaines, IL 60018
Allow four to six weeks for delivery.
Prices and availability subject to change without notice.   FN143 7/94

Bestselling Women's Fiction

Sandra Brown

_____	28951-9 TEXAS! LUCKY	$5.99/6.99 in Canada
_____	28990-X TEXAS! CHASE	$5.99/6.99
_____	29500-4 TEXAS! SAGE	$5.99/6.99
_____	29085-1 22 INDIGO PLACE	$5.99/6.99
_____	29783-X A WHOLE NEW LIGHT	$5.99/6.99
_____	56045-X TEMPERATURES RISING	$5.99/6.99
_____	56274-6 FANTA C	$4.99/5.99
_____	56278-9 LONG TIME COMING	$4.99/5.99

Amanda Quick

_____	28354-5 SEDUCTION	$5.99/6.99
_____	28932-2 SCANDAL	$5.99/6.99
_____	28594-7 SURRENDER	$5.99/6.99
_____	29325-7 RENDEZVOUS	$5.99/6.99
_____	29316-8 RECKLESS	$5.99/6.99
_____	29316-8 RAVISHED	$4.99/5.99
_____	29317-6 DANGEROUS	$5.99/6.99
_____	56506-0 DECEPTION	$5.99/7.50

Nora Roberts

_____	29078-9 GENUINE LIES	$5.99/6.99
_____	28578-5 PUBLIC SECRETS	$5.99/6.99
_____	26461-3 HOT ICE	$5.99/6.99
_____	26574-1 SACRED SINS	$5.99/6.99
_____	27859-2 SWEET REVENGE	$5.99/6.99
_____	27283-7 BRAZEN VIRTUE	$5.99/6.99
_____	29597-7 CARNAL INNOCENCE	$5.50/6.50
_____	29490-3 DIVINE EVIL	$5.99/6.99

Iris Johansen

_____	29871-2 LAST BRIDGE HOME	$4.50/5.50
_____	29604-3 THE GOLDEN BARBARIAN	$4.99/5.99
_____	29244-7 REAP THE WIND	$4.99/5.99
_____	29032-0 STORM WINDS	$4.99/5.99
_____	28855-5 THE WIND DANCER	$4.95/5.95
_____	29968-9 THE TIGER PRINCE	$5.50/6.50
_____	29944-1 THE MAGNIFICENT ROGUE	$5.99/6.99
_____	29945-X BELOVED SCOUNDREL	$5.99/6.99

Ask for these titles at your bookstore or use this page to order.

Please send me the books I have checked above. I am enclosing $ _____ (add $2.50 to cover postage and handling). Send check or money order, no cash or C. O. D.'s please.

Mr./ Ms. _____

Address _____

City/ State/ Zip _____

Send order to: Bantam Books, Dept. FN 16, 2451 S. Wolf Road, Des Plaines, IL 60018

Please allow four to six weeks for delivery.

Prices and availability subject to change without notice.   FN 16 - 4/94